MW01136436

Chasing Fireflies

by Claudia Burgoa

Copyright © 2019 by Claudia Burgoa

Cover by: By Hang Le
Edited by: Paulina Burgoa
Dannielle Leigh Editorial

All rights reserved. No part of this publication may be reproduced, transmitted, downloaded, distributed, stored in or introduced into any information storage and retrieval system, in any form or by any means, whether electronic, photocopying, mechanical or otherwise, without express permission of the publisher, except by a reviewer who may quote brief passages for review purposes.
This book is a work of fiction. Names, characters, brands, media, places, storylines and incidents are the product of the author's imagination or are used fictitiously. Any resemblance to any person, living or dead, or any events or occurrences, is purely coincidental.
The author acknowledges the trademarked status and trademark owners of various products, brands, and-or restaurants referenced in this work of fiction, of which have been used without permission. The use of these trademarks is not authorized with or sponsored by the trademark owners.

Also by Claudia Burgoa

Uncut

Undefeated

Decker the Halls

"I believe that all of our lives we're looking for home and if we're really lucky, we find it in someone's loving arms. I think that' what life is-coming home." –Anita Krizzan

To the South

Before ...

ONE

Kaitlynn

IN THE BEGINNING, there were fireflies, crisp floating dots wading through the summer breeze.

There were children in the streets and popsicles being passed out by a local grandmother. There were skinned knees, too much sunscreen, and the wafting scent of freshly cut grass. There were long days and even longer nights.

Summers in Knox Ridge were just as much about mosquito nets and cicada songs as they were about lemonade and sunshine.

Knox Ridge wasn't the biggest town in Georgia, but there were too many of us to learn each other's names by heart. Most people grew up on the same street their parents did all those years ago.

They grew from a twinkle in their parents' eyes to people who would one day take their places in the layout of our town. Their legacies cast shadows on every succeeding generation—what they'd do, where they lived, and who they loved. The town had a blueprint most didn't question, but also didn't consider too much.

"Being a part of Knox Ridge was a privilege," my Nana used to say.

It was a privilege to live around people who genuinely care for you and an honor to have a place like Knox Ridge to come home to.

"Every town on Earth says they're the best," Nana always said. "But how many towns can say 'if you're with us, we'll accept every part of you?'"

Only Knox Ridge.

She swore that no one truly left Knox Ridge once they'd gotten a taste of living here, but some took breaks. She was right, some people drifted in and out of our sleepy town, but they always came back home. Even if they hadn't realized they'd left.

I met Oliver Tanner one blistering afternoon in July.

He was five years old, moving back into the childhood home of his recently deceased father. I was four, sitting next door on my front porch with my best friend, Paige, munching on watermelon as we did nearly every afternoon.

Paige's father had been my father's best friend since childhood. As I said, there was a blueprint to this town.

Oliver wore ripped cargo shorts and clenched a dinosaur toy tightly to his chest. I had never seen anyone in that house. Not until they arrived.

"I never thought I'd live to see another Tanner live in that house," my grandmother said.

I wouldn't learn until years later the tumultuous history of the Tanner family in town. Once one of the most respected families of Knox Ridge, Oliver's grandfather had left them disgraced and destitute three decades earlier when he ran off to California with a woman he barely knew. The Tanner's had been in a downward spiral ever since.

"Well come on, sweeties," my grandmother nudged Paige and myself. "Let's go say hello. See if they need anything. That girl doesn't look a day over twenty."

Nana had been more or less right. Josey Tanner was twenty-five, freshly widowed, and out of money from living out west. Her only option was moving to this house she'd inherited from her husband's passing and spreading out his meager life insurance for as long as she could.

Nana introduced us to Oliver and his mother. Josey likewise introduced him to us.

"You got movers to help you with that truck?" Nana asked.

"No," Josey said.

"Are you renting it by the hour or the day?"

"Day," she answered. "I've got it rented for the whole week."

Nana nodded before waving them both over. "No use doing anything now, then. Come over for some lemonade. My sons get off work at about five. They'll wrangle up some friends to do it for you."

That day was one of my first memories of Nana being Nana, pulling people together for the common good as she always did.

"Now you two be nice to the Tanner boy," Nana told Paige and me. "He looks like he could use a bit of TLC."

That day was also the day Ollie was entrusted to my keep. He was a year older than me, but back in those days, he was as large and loud as a church mouse. His sandy blonde hair stuck up in ways that defied gravity, and he mostly muttered as we asked him about his dinosaurs.

We dragged him out back where all the magic happened, spending hours in the sun as the clouds and world passed us by. Our parents filtered in and out to keep an eye on us.

When the sun started to go down, and the fireflies started to peek out from their slumber, it was like his whole face lit up. I think that was the first time I knew I never wanted to stop looking at that smile.

"What are those?" he asked.

"For Christ's sake, haven't you ever seen a firefly before?"

Paige asked, ever the spitting image of her father; who had too little patience for others.

He shrugged, smile faltering. It broke my heart before I was even old enough to know that was possible. Something about him made me want to protect him from everything.

I took his hand in mine. "Let's catch some," I said. "We'll show you."

"Fireflies knew how to call each other back home," I told him like Nana had taught me. "They danced and flickered to the rhythm of their love song."

Nana taught me a lot. Like how fireflies were magic with the persistence of a person, that's what I loved about them. No matter how far they strayed, they remembered where they came from and who their family was. They always took my breath away.

Nana shouted for us to grab our firefly jars, each equipped with air holes at the top, courtesy of my dad's power drill.

Paige took some joy in bossing Ollie around, telling him he was doing it wrong at every turn. But I took pity on him, reminding her that Nana was watching.

The fireflies danced all around us, enchanting Ollie into a stupor. Once we'd caught a few, we went chasing after the others just for the fun of it. His laugh was brighter than the sun. It was so special that my brain never let me forget it.

We got lost in the magic of the night and the fireflies. It wasn't until Josey came back to call us that I realized I had been up past my bedtime. As an exception, Mom let me go to Ollie's house to say goodnight. After all, it was a special night.

Holding hands, I took the jar of fireflies up to Ollie's room with him.

"Here," I said proudly as I set it on the nightstand. "Now you'll have friends to help you sleep. But let 'em go tomorrow alright? They have to go home."

Years later, Josey told me that's the moment when she realized she had made the right decision by moving to Knox Ridge.

But back then, in the quiet shelter of a new friend's bedroom that was still littered in half opened boxes and clutter—all I could see was the smile on Ollie's face.

A FEW SUMMERS LATER, the sun had crept past us a few times. We were taller, louder, and more self-assured.

Josey had tried her hand at a few odd jobs around town until my parents hired her as a waitress. That had been almost two years prior. Lots of things had changed in that time, but some things seemed doomed to stay the same.

The town was still sleepy from the summer that stretched as far back as April and reached deep into October. The Nelson twins were keeping a bug collection in their closet that got them grounded for most of the summer—again. Britney Jones broke her arm that summer when she tried to help Duncan Foster with his broken knee (don't ask me how).

Mr. Woods on the next block bought a new lawnmower that sent him into a gardening war with Ms. Schaffer like nothing the town had seen in years. Nana would have to intervene when those fights got out of hand. People loved her and sometimes feared her too.

Of course, her meddling included matchmaking. Ms. Schaffer and Mr. Woods would go on to marry three years later, to the surprise of no one. Nana also tried her hand at some new cobbler recipes, for better or worse.

Uncle Jim, who still spoke to us back then, was delighted to try every flavor she came up with—even the infamous lemon banana pecan crumble. We never spoke of it after that day.

Paige's father didn't come home enough from his life as a truck driver, but he always sent postcards. Her mom worked as a flight attendant, so Paige spent most weekdays being shuttled between her grandmother's house and Nana's.

Our family restaurant was as busy as ever. At least, too busy to keep an eye on us while we played in the backyard behind the Victorian house the restaurant occupied. And my older sister Kelsey was the same as ever.

"Hey dummies," Kelsey screamed at Ollie and me one blistering June afternoon the year I turned eight. "Stop running and pay attention to me!"

Ollie and I had been playing knights of Camelot, as we did back in those days. He rolled his eyes dramatically as he turned around to ask her what she wanted.

"I'm bored and mom said you have to play with me," she said.

"No she didn't," I said.

Mom never forced us to play.

"Well, she told me to find something fun to do so shut your faces and come here. We're going to play a game," Kelsey said.

"We're already playing knights," Ollie claimed. He wasn't a fan of my sister.

Kelsey glared at us for a second.

"Fine," she said finally. "We can play make-believe like a bunch of babies."

"We're not—"

"Shut it, Kaitlynn," she snapped at me. "Or I'll tell Dad what happened to his rock collection."

Olli and I shared a smile. Some were at the bottom of the lake; others were now part of my pet rock collection.

Kelsey was so bossy and mean back in those days. Nana used to say that you only had to look at someone's childhood, their rearing and home, to understand why their heart grew into what it is now. It never made sense to me where Kelsey was concerned.

We had the same rearing, home, and practically the same exact childhood. But I never understood what turned her into such a vindictive brat. I'd like to say that life is filled with people who grow and get over their past transgressions.

"Come on, frogface!" Kelsey shouted. "I'll be the Fairy Godmother and you'll be the ugly princess I turned into a dragon. Oliver can be the knight that slays you."

But some people never move past certain stages of their life. Kelsey would grow more beautiful with every year, but humility and kindness were never her strong suits.

"That's a stupid game," Ollie said. "Kit Kat isn't ugly—"

My cheek went red any time he said something nice about me.

"—And she's too easy to slay," he said. "We'd be done too fast."

I stuck my tongue out at him. "Says you."

I chased after him, Kelsey's game was mostly forgotten. The tall grass brushed against us as we ran toward the sunset—or toward the back fence. Or both.

Clouds skimmed the periphery of our kingdom, greeting us as we charged to our "destiny" and each other. We tackled and ran after each other across the yard, laughter drowning out Kelsey's protests.

There was so much beauty in the world back in those days. Maybe it was just the optimism of youth tricking our eyes into seeing a better world than there was. But with the dirt under our feet, faces in the crisp breeze, and souls locked into the heartbeat of Knox Ridge—anything seemed possible.

We would stay there, in that loving trance of naivety, long into the twilight of our childhood. We fought and played in an eternal dance around each other. Like our fireflies, we were chasing each other to the horizon.

"You two are such losers," Kelsey said that day like she did most afternoons.

It didn't matter, though. We hardly ever listened to her in those days.

KIDS WERE CRUEL. Looking back, I'm not sure if there was ever a way out of that phenomena. Kids were excited, everything was different, including their emotions.

So, when kids started to understand what made them different from each other, and how unsettling that could feel, they clung to it for all the wrong reasons.

Poor kids were bound to get picked on more in Knox Ridge. None of us were rich like the families up in Atlanta. But kids would always notice the difference between the have-somes and the have-nots.

Every year like clockwork, the middle schoolers had a new trend to follow. Anyone who didn't fit the mold was interrogated, and then ostracized when it was revealed that they couldn't afford to buy into that trend.

Ollie's crucifixion came with a wave of digital watches that were so gaudy, only a teenage boy would like them. He carpooled with us on a Monday in September, wading into a sea of screaming boys arguing over who had the best watch.

Monday, he had his friends and regular lunch table. By Wednesday, most of them were shrugging him off about after school plans. By Friday, he was sitting with Paige and me underneath the bleachers of the track field.

Paige liked sitting there so she could be outside without burning her "delicate" skin. I preferred outside to the cacophony of pre-teens shouting inside the cafeteria.

We didn't ask questions when Ollie found us that afternoon, glaring at his food while he silently dug into it. But things were different. Life has shifted in a blink of an eye.

Ollie was already treated differently by the kids in town because he had a single mom. This was back in the days where a "failed" marriage still left a dent in anyone's reputation. Adults and kids didn't care that Ollie's dad had died.

It was all the same to them—Josey should've gotten remarried as far as they were concerned. If she didn't want to be "lonely" or "pathetic," she should've gotten a new husband by now.

Rumors of his father's death spread every year or so back then.

Kids came up with increasingly elaborate and offensive stories of Mr. Tanner's untimely passing. None of them cared what that did to Ollie. These kids were vain and shortsighted. They didn't understand what they were doing to him or what they were missing by not being his friend.

They didn't see how bright and imaginative he was. They didn't realize how much love he had in his life because he always went the extra mile.

"Look, guys," Jenkins said to his cronies as they crashed our group one day at lunch. "Tanner's so poor, he needs his little girlfriend to give him lunch."

Ollie sat there, frozen in silence.

Jenkins laughed. "What's the matter, Tanner? Too hungry to talk back?"

"Fuck off, Jenkins," I said.

Adam Jenkins III was from Connecticut by birth and never let anyone forget that. His mom was once a model in New York, and he had bright blue eyes to show for it. Unfortunately for everyone, his nose was naturally turned up so high that he gave "snot-nosed" a whole new meaning.

Jenkins laughed at me.

"What are you gonna do, Blythe? Go tell to your sister on me?"

Kelsey had a penchant for roughing people up when someone pissed her off. Jenkins was just too dumb to realize that it was genetic.

A second later, his nose cracked easily under the pressure of my fist. To this day, he claims the only reason I was able to punch him at that moment is because I caught him off guard. I couldn't find it in my heart to feel bad when he came into school a few months later with a better looking nose.

Ollie wasn't grateful for my "interfering," however.

"You shouldn't have done that," he told me while walking to his mom's car that day.

"What was I supposed to do? Sit there and do nothing?"

"I don't need you fighting for me," Ollie said. "I don't need some girl making me look like a wimp in front of everyone."

His words hurt me, but I understood where he was coming from. He had been told left and right for years that he wasn't good enough because his family wasn't. Now they could tell him he wasn't good enough because of something directly about him.

He could have fought back, but I didn't let him.

But that's the thing, Ollie didn't fight back.

I could see how trapped he felt in front of that group of boys, and I knew it wasn't going to end well. What was my other option? Let him get beat up right in front of me?

Jenkins didn't have the balls to hit a girl and, as Nana would later tell me during my grounding, that was Jenkins's problem. Not mine.

Maybe I was wrong to hit him, maybe, but I saw someone who needed help and I did something about it. That's how my parents raised me.

Mom always told me that the difference between helping and

hurting is a fine line. That forcing help on someone is the quickest way to lose someone's trust and friendship.

Where did that leave me? I was stuck feeling vulnerable and in trouble with my best friend.

"Well tough, okay?" I said defensively. "You're my friend. You're a good person. You deserve better than those assfaces giving you shit."

He stared at me for a second before throwing the car door open. He didn't say anything but...it was the first time I felt like he really saw me.

TWO

Oliver

GROWING up in Knox Ridge was an experience I didn't appreciate until it was too late.

It was the kind of town where everyone was your neighbor, for better or worse. As a teenager, I felt the effects of "or worse" more often than not. My mom was a hard-working woman, had been her entire life.

She raised me to work hard, and to listen harder. She taught me the value of an education had obvious benefits, like better job prospects and a higher salary, were important but the merit of an education is something no one could take away from me.

Unfortunately, I didn't understand that lesson until years later. When I was in junior high, I took the education I received for granted. Intelligence was for nerds back then, and as one of the poorer kids at school, I couldn't afford to have another strike against me.

I picked up a sport after school in seventh grade as an attempt to take some of the heat off me from local bullies, as well as to build muscle. That's how I ended up dedicating most of my spare time to perfecting my baseball pitch. Which included volunteering my best friend to be my batter.

Kaitlynn Blythe wasn't a tomboy by any stretch of the imagination. She wore pink and kept her hair in braids when her mother had time or her sister had an itch to play with hair. Her other best friend at the time, Paige, was as girly as they came and those two got along better than we did sometimes.

Regardless, Kaitlynn humored me most lunches and afternoons. Sometimes she'd do homework in the library after school or sit in on a play rehearsal when Paige or Kelsey were starring in one. But most of the fall and winter for two years was the two of us practicing out behind the school. I'd pitch to her and she'd try to aim for the fence behind me.

"You're getting pretty good at this," I told her the afternoon of her thirteenth birthday. "You could be a pro if you wanted. Put Mark McGwire in his place."

She blushed, shrugging as she stared at her bat. "It's not so hard if I pretend the ball is your face."

I laughed so hard, I forgot to breathe. She knew how to keep me humble.

"C'mon," she said impatiently. "We've got enough time for a few more pitches."

I shrugged, letting the ball slip from my mitt. Kaitlynn had this habit of putting what I wanted above her own desires. I took that for granted a lot in those days. But that afternoon with the leaves rustling and her long auburn hair out waving just like the trees, the sun hit her just right as she smiled shyly.

"What?" she asked as she nervously shifted from side to side.

She was so good, one of the best people I had, or would ever, meet. She talked a lot and was sometimes too friendly for her own good, but she fought hard for everything she had. She was passionate about everything she loved and had this sense of self awareness that most people would never understand. She was radically honest and unapologetic about being herself.

She was everything I wished I could be, and then some.

It was the first time looking at her made me forget how to speak. It was also the first time I realized she should ask for more than she accepted.

"Wanna go somewhere?" I said. "It's your birthday."

"Like...where?" she asked.

I shrugged. "Wherever, c'mon."

I convinced her to hop on my bike and we ended up sitting in a nearby creek with a carton of ice cream from the convenience store. The water was getting colder with fall encroaching, but we dipped our feet in anyway.

Word spreads fast in a small town, unfortunately. Her mother found out by dinner and almost took away our cake privileges because of it.

Sitting side by side in that creek, though, we laughed about childish things. Her head ended up on my shoulder as we talked about the forts we could build out there next summer.

"Thanks," she whispered. "This was the best birthday ever."

Nothing else mattered there.

It was just us.

And the world was more beautiful because of it.

"Anything for you, Kit Kat," I said.

I was too young to realize how much I meant that, and much too naive to realize it would be many years until I could keep that promise.

WHEN I GOT to the ripe old age of fourteen, my mom started working a second job across town to try to save for my college. The

Blythe's, being the kind of people they were, took on my care even more after that point.

They'd always given my mother an extra hand where they could. I guess I should've seen it coming with two jobs when dinners with my mom got fewer and farther apart.

The spring of my freshman year of high school, I sat at the Blythe's dinner table more often than not. I knew the routine, be inside by 5 pm, grab the silverware, and help set the table with Kelsey. Kelsey always found a reason to be dissatisfied with my place settings, so eventually I was put on dish duty after dinner instead.

The Blythe's home wasn't any bigger than my own, but in terms of love it had us beat. Mr. and Mrs. Blythe flirted with each other like newlyweds while Nana Blythe chided them. Paige and Kaitlynn helped Nana with dinner more and more as we got older.

Every person in that house had a role to play and the space to make it their own. But it never felt the same for me, the kid of an absent single mom. As an adult, I would love and cherish every moment she sacrificed to give me the kind of life where I could thrive.

But as a child, all I could see were the moments we lost, the conversations we didn't have anymore, and the distance between us.

Some days I was able to push past it because I still had the Blythes. But some days, nothing could keep me from focusing on the mom-sized hole in my heart.

Life never stayed still, even when the town did. One day, without any notice, my best friend lost one of the most important people in her life. Nana. I hugged her as she cried. Mom let me stay over with her for a couple of nights because Kaitlynn was incon-solable.

The entire town mourned. We have lost a piece of our hearts.

Everyone in town had a connection with her. She was the soul and the glue that kept Knox Ridge together.

One night, a few weeks after her death, all came to ahead. The wound was still fresh from her passing and the whole house fell silent because of it. Dinners were a quiet, desolate affair unlike anything they'd been before.

Of course it was. We lost Nana. She was the biggest voice in the house. Then, suddenly, one morning...she didn't wake.

She left us completely out of my element. I hadn't felt this alone since Dad died. For the first time in my life, I felt like no one was in my corner.

"Son, can you pass me the peas?" Richard Blythe, Kaitlynn's dad asked.

It was a simple request but ...

"I'm not your son," I snapped.

I wasn't anything to them. My mother had abandoned me with this family who could just kick me out because I wasn't part of them. The only other person who had cared for me had left me.

Richard and his wife, Cynthia, gaped at me. It made my ears burn red in embarrassment, but that only stoked the fire of my rage.

"Alright, Ollie," she said. "Could you please pass—"

"My name isn't Ollie, it's fucking Oliver okay? I'm not some fucking child—"

Richard frowned. "Young man you better watch your language—"

I didn't mean what I said next. Even now, I feel the sting of cruelty and flinch at the pain in their eyes as I held everything against them: the years of bullying, the empty house I was forced to sleep in, the judgmental looks every ballgame when Richard showed up instead of someone else, the disappointing family func-tions...even Nana's death.

None of it was their fault, but I felt the weight of it all breaking me. Someone had to feel it too. I couldn't be alone in this. So... I lashed out.

"Or what? You'll ground me? Newsflash, you are not my parents," I shouted. "You're just some assholes who get off on taking pity for charity cases."

Cynthia stood up, "Go to your room."

I sputtered. It wasn't even my house. "But—"

"March yourself right on over to your room this instant, Oliver Hugh Tanner," she pointed at the door. "I will be calling your mama. You will be grounded, and you *will* finish your dinner when you remember your manners."

I practically threw my chair as I got up, taking heavy steps toward the door. Those steps were as angry and vengeful as I felt. *How dare they refuse to take shit from me?* I thought at the time.

I was still pissed off when I finally made it to my second-floor bedroom next door. Anger was rolling off me as I clenched my pillow and screamed into it. I was so angry at the world and the life I'd been forced into living.

I was so sick of being treated like a freak and failure for things that were outside of my control. I was so frustrated that one of the only constants in my life, my next-door neighbor's grandmother of all people, had been ripped away from me.

Did anyone care what I thought?

Did no one realize I'd lost her too?

My screams devolved into tears.

Who would be there for me now? I kept asking myself. *Would anyone miss me when I was gone?*

Someone knocked on my door a while later. I mumbled, "come in," through swollen eyes and chapped lips. The bed dipped as a hand rubbed my shoulder.

"What's going on, sweetie?" Cynthia asked me.

"Everything sucks," I said, because I didn't know how to articu-

17

late what was wrong.

She squeezed my shoulder. "Is that all?"

"This town sucks," I continued, sniffing. "Everyone either hates me or forgets I exist."

"That's not true. We love you, and so does your mom—"

"Then where is she?" my voice cracked through a sob. "Where was she when Nana died? She doesn't even care."

"Oh, honey," she said. "C'mon, sit up. You need a hug."

She held me tightly as I sobbed into her shoulder.

"She loves you so very much. She is trying her hardest to give you everything you deserve just on her own," Cynthia explained. "You've just gotta be a little patient and remember that whenever she isn't here, she's out doing things for you."

"Doesn't stop everyone from calling me a fucking orphan," I said.

She nodded as she hugged me harder. We sat there a while in silence.

"I know being a Blythe is hard," she said finally.

"I'm not a Blythe," I said.

"Honey I hate to break it to you, but you've been a Blythe since you were five years old and everyone in this town knows it. Nana took one look at you and knew you and your mama were meant to be right here, with us."

The thought of Nana accepting us even back then, made my throat tight with grief.

She sighed. "Unfortunately, being a Blythe in this town means everyone expects the world of you. That goes double for a Blythe that's been adopted into the fold. Believe me, every girl in town hated my guts when the realized I wasn't just another waitress at *Blythe's*."

"Is that supposed to make me feel better," I muttered.

Cynthia laughed sadly. "Guess not, but misery loves company, right?"

I laughed. "Yeah."

She squeezed me one more time before moving back. She fixed my hair and wiped away my tears. Cynthia looked me squarely in the eyes with the kind of determination that could only come from a mother's love. For the first time since Nana's death, I didn't feel so alone.

Then she said something I would never forget.

"Maybe we're not what you wanted or had in mind when you imagined your life. But we're what you've got. And we love you, alright? Don't push away the people who love you. You're hurting? Let us help carry the load."

THE BLYTHES LOVED TYBEE ISLAND. Every summer, they would close down the restaurant for a week or two, pack up their family and close friends, and head down to a house they rented from a cousin at a discount.

The house in question had built a dock out to the beach in the late 80s before they became illegal. It was one of the best spots in all of Georgia.

Going to Tybee was normally reserved for August. When the sky was blazing from the summer sun and everything seemed to stand still because of the intense heat, that's when we knew it was time to head to Tybee.

The drive was always filled with frequent stops, games of I Spy, and more singing than I cared to hear. The annual trip to Tybee Island was one of the only times a year we could get Paige's parents and my mom to take time off from work. For a brief moment once a year, everyone was together without a care in the world.

The summer after I turned 15 was no exception. Paige and

Kelsey spent most of the day tanning on the beach. Paige's dad, Arthur, and Richard would oscillate between throwing a football around, grilling, and trying not to overdo it on body surfing.

Their wives would keep an eye on them when they were at the house but spent most of their time in town, whether they were drinking or shopping or both I never knew for sure.

Kaitlynn and I spent most of those days, especially as teenagers, biking anywhere the wind would take us. We spent hours following every twist and turn on that island. We'd sit on the beach and people watch until we were bored enough to people watch as we cruised past the other rental houses.

On this trip in particular, we were conned into babysitting for a couple from Knox Ridge in return for use of their jet ski. We spent half day on the beach building sandcastles with a four and a six-year-old boys.

The kids even went as far as to bury me in the sand, with Kaitlynn's help. But the feeling of cutting through waves on that jet ski made it all worth it.

With the wind rushing against us and Kaitlynn's arms wrapped around me tight, I felt invincible. We took that jet ski so far along the cost, I hardly remembered where we'd come from both literally and existentially.

Nothing mattered in that sea but feeling free with Kaitlynn by my side. She was the kind of person who laughed when she was the right kind of scared. She laughed at every wave that jostled us.

Her laughs reminded me to be careful, but they also energized me. There was something so perfect about being out there and all I could think about was how I never wanted it to end.

"Stop," she said eventually.

I slowed the jet ski down. "Why?"

"You ever considered enjoying the view?"

I looked over my shoulder, smirking at her. "I am."

She rolled her eyes. "Seriously, Ollie, look at this place."

My eyes scanned every inch of our view. "Okay?"

"No, seriously, look," she said. "Everything for miles and miles is just beach and water. It's nature uninterrupted. Don't you see how beautiful that is? We're part of this ... giant ecosystem. We could be down there, somewhere at the bottom of the ocean but we're not. We're up here doing whatever we please."

I took another glance for her sake. I understood what she meant that time. Feeling so calm and at ease with being a small part of a larger cosmos. The water was everything—life and death, energy and stillness, light and dark. We were part of something bigger than we could fully comprehend.

My breath caught as she gripped me tighter.

"Beautiful, right?" she said.

I nodded.

Kit Kat had an artist's eye when it came to the world. From every angle, she could see a canvas adorned in colors and motion that most of us could only hope to see. The world was more than pain and disappointment in her eyes.

It was beautiful and she was just as beautiful for realizing it.

"Yeah," I said. "Really beautiful."

We sat there for a while drinking up the sun and pulse of the sea for as long as we could. The world was bigger than my own backyard, I realized that day. I vowed to see every inch of it if possible, starting with everything just beyond the Atlantic.

"C'mon," Kaitlynn said eventually. "Let's turn around before we end up washing up on the shore of Hilton Head."

I never told her how much that afternoon meant to me, sitting there with her, with the world and our whole lives ahead of us and her being as calm as the sea. But maybe someday I would get up the nerve to tell her how much her laugh and wit fills everything she touches with love.

Chapter Three

Fourteen years ago

Ollie,

Greetings from chef camp!

I still get chills saying that.

The Junior Culinary Intensive is everything I could've hoped for and more. You know cooking hasn't been the same without Nana. But things feel so right here. I was worried about being bad compared to these hot shot teen chefs. I'm doing way better than I expected and it's just a dream.

I don't know if I'd be as well adjusted if it weren't for Paige, though. She's really been my rock here. She says hi, by the way. And she made me promise to tell you, "Don't forget to wear sunscreen on lifeguard duty, dipshit." See? She does care, lol.

How are things going at home? You holding down the fort alright at the restaurant? Hope Kelsey isn't putting all the obnoxious tourists in your section! I'm so thankful that you're there to keep Mom and Dad sane, we know that isn't Kelsey's strong suit. I know they were worried that 15 is too young for

Paige and me to be off in Rhode Island like this, but we're having a blast.

Besides, we're using up so much energy that we couldn't go sneaking out after curfew even if we wanted to.

Thanks again for being your awesome self. I hope you enjoy the "reject" shortcakes Paige and I made last week. More "bad" pastries to follow.

Love,

Kaitlynn

KIT KAT,

Another update from pool life:

Mrs. Abernathy is having a midlife crisis and so is Dr. Renner. Am I allowed to ban people from the pool until they get over their weird sexual tension? It's bad enough I have to see Dr. Renner awkwardly flirt about Vitamin D deficiencies.

In other news, Kelsey's dating some guy with a "boat house." Not a lake house, and it's not his parents. He's building a fucking house out of an old yacht he salvaged from a junkyard. His parents are in town for the summer doing some sort of development project. So at least he isn't weird, dumb, and too old for her.

Anyway, Blythe's is fine. I know you ask every other week, but your parents are fine. Yeah, they miss you, but why wouldn't they?

They're your parents.

Mom said thanks for those "faulty" croissants. She says she hopes your instructor "finds someone to remove that stick from his ass." She also said "take a cheap ticket and go see Boston for a day or two...Don't tell your parents this was my idea. But live a little."

So there you have it, if you get grounded this summer it'll be my mom's fault and I'll get grounded for enabling you. But you know *what? It's worth it. Go live your life, try not to get in too much trouble.*

Yours,

Oliver 'off duty' Tanner

OLLIE,

Are you kidding me? How did Joel Henderson even GET that close to the quarry? And where did the racoon come from? I swear that town falls apart any time I leave for more than a few days. People are obnoxious up here.

At first, I didn't really notice it because I'm so new. But holy f*ck, they aren't kidding about "Southern Hospitality." People stare when I say more than three words to a cashier. INCLUDING the cashiers.

There goes my dream of working in a New York bakery. Maybe someday? Paige still loves it here. I swear she didn't even know what a c*nt was until we got here. Now she won't stop saying it.

It's like all I here now, unless she adds the word b*tch :/

The intensive course is still going well. We're working more on knife skills right now. Attached, as requested, I've included a few pictures of our knicks and bandages. I don't understand why Tommy Schmidt wants these but remember we each get 30% of the cut.

Hope all is well with you.

Wishing you a safer summer than mine,

Kaitlynn "Skidmark" Blythe

Kit Kat,

Don't ask where the racoon came from. Your parents are already suing the hardware store, leave it at that. Shit's always crazy here. I think it's just more noticeable when you're in the middle of it.

Hospitality...

Remember, not everyone's going to be as nice as you.

What are you going to do when you get invited to guest chef all over the world?

Say "no I can't, people will stare at me if I talk to your cashiers?"

You're kidding me right? Paige has a dirtier mouth than her dad. Remember when I was nine and, uh, "borrowed" her skateboard? She found me and screamed, "hey jackass, give it back right now before I rip your dick off."

Tommy said "thanks, keep 'em coming." Attached to this letter is your cut of the revenue. 30% each just like we agreed. He also asked for "pictures of water, bells, and pigeons." Whatever that means.

Kelsey's dating Arnold Foston, again. I'd feel bad for that guy if I didn't know what he did last year in the locker room after baseball practice.

Here's hoping you have a more carefree summer than that.

YOURS,

Oliver "Still Queasy" Tanner

OLLIE,

How are you? My week is going SWELL. Paige almost broke her arm showing off to a California boy and the dickweed from Wyoming won't stop asking me about bugs. Do I look like a bug expert?

I swear all the good guys here either already have girlfriends or were snatched up weeks ago. Just as well, I don't think anyone would believe me if I came back from Rhode Island saying "I had this hot boyfriend from Milwaukee," or "Yeah I was seeing this dude from Eugene, Oregon, but we're in different time zones so ~~shit~~ fell apart."

Don't tell my parents I said "shit."

How are you? Is your mom still dating that guy from Macon? Did that sunburn clear up alright? Paige says, "I told you so," by the way.

YOURS,

    Kaitlynn "Forever Single" Blythe

KIT KAT,

    Well your dad finally caved today. He drove me forty miles out to a DMV that doesn't remember last year's parallel parking debacle. I still think Joel should've gotten detention for that. It isn't my fault that I didn't know what he did to his car when I borrowed it.

    So now you're looking at a fully licensed driver! Only four months behind schedule.

    I think it was Britney Jones' party that sent your parents over the edge.

    On an unrelated note...guess who's grounded for three weeks? And guess who's skinning potatoes for six?

    How goes the coffee tour of New England? Did Paige ever make headway with that guy from the cheese class?

    Yours,

    Oliver "Grounded for Life" Tanner

OLLIE,

We're leaving on Sunday and I can't believe this summer has flown by so quickly. Thanks again for all the awesome updates along the way. In case this gets to you before we return home, I want you to know how much I've missed you and can't wait to see you again. And in case this gets there after we do—you still owe me for that shit from Salem you made me buy.

Until we meet again, I hope you keep your head up and your eyes on the prize (or horizon...I don't know which sounds better).

Always Yours,

Kit Kat

FOUR

Oliver

WHEN I WAS in high school, my mom tore her ACL at her second job. She got workman's comp and between that and our savings we made it by for a while. Paying for physical therapy ate at what money we were getting.

The Blythe's helped and loaned money when they could but after a few months of struggling, I had to ask them for a job to help cover the bills.

I was extremely thankful and lucky that they paid me full time hours to work on a part time schedule.

"Your morning shift is going to school, alright?" Cynthia said to me. "All of our staff need at least a high school education to work here. So make sure school stays your priority, young man."

Working at Blythe's was surreal. I grew up running around out back and occasionally helping with the dishes. Waiting during the summer and doing it on weekdays and weekends was a whole different animal.

Weeknights weren't as crazy as weekends, but it was still

chaotic juggling multiple tasks at once. It taught me a lot about discipline and perseverance.

Blythe's was alive back in those days. Every hour, there were locals filtering in with cheerful greetings and empty stomachs ready to be filled. Richard and Cynthia made an effort to visit with every table we served every day, especially the families.

"We're not just serving food," Richard would say. "We're serving hospitality and an experience. People could go to any restaurant in town for decent food, but they come to Blythe's for great food and great people. Customers come back because they know we care if they do or don't."

When Nana was still alive, she would add, "Plus they're vultures who hate to be behind on the latest gossip. You know what's the easiest way to get news in Knox Ridge? Go to Blythe's."

Blythe's was supposed to be everything that made home cooking wonderful with the convenience of going out to eat. They did that tenfold, not just through service but with how the dining area was set up.

All the tables had been custom made fifty years ago from trees from a nearby forest. The floors were plush carpet that, despite being installed twenty years before, were still in pretty good shape. The paint and art on the walls, accumulated from generations of the family and contributions from the town, made it feel like eating in someone's home.

That's what made Blythe's so special. People came to dine with the Blythes and they were never disappointed.

Most nights, I would get back to my house around 11 pm, 10 pm if it was a slow night or the Blythe's let me go early because of an exam the next morning. The first floor was typically dark and slumbering when I arrived.

Unlike the first floor, upstairs was normally lit, and laughter would filter from my mother's room to every corner of the house. I would trudge up the stairs tiredly every night, shuck my things in my room, and then quietly head to mom's room.

Kaitlynn had taken it upon herself to take care of Mom while I was at work. She would cook dinner and enough leftovers for my lunch the next day. She helped Mom get around when she needed to and kept her company as she did her homework.

Some days, I would find Paige watching a movie with them, but I knew I could always count on Kaitlynn. She never asked for anything in return, even the few times I tried to pay her back for all the care she gave my mom.

"Family helps family, alright?" she said one time. "I'm just doing my job and I'm happy to do it."

Every night I would find Mom and Kaitlynn giggling like they were best friends, and every time it would do something to my heart. It was like an awkward stutter that made my chest warm and kept me thinking about her at night.

I didn't understand what any of that meant. Years later, I would regret how oblivious I had been in high school.

"Alright anyone who isn't a Tanner should tumble back home," I would say most nights.

Kaitlynn would roll her eyes. "You think you're hilarious," she'd say every so often as she held back a smile.

I would say goodnight to my mom as Kaitlynn packed up her things. Then I'd walk Kaitlynn to her door, which wasn't far but I still insisted on making sure she got home safe.

In hindsight, I could've kissed her any one of those nights— when the moon was shining, when the leaves were flying all around us, or even in the rain.

I could have let her step inside before I knocked on the door to ask her for a date. I could have kissed her behind her parents' restaurant any of the times we watched the sunset out there. I could have kissed her while we laid by the creek.

I could have taken her on a date so many times or told her how much she took my breath away or even told her how beautiful she was.

But I didn't.

So every night for almost two years, I walked her from my mother's bed to her front door. 236 feet that I could have used to tell her how much I cared about her.

Instead, most nights ended with an awkward shrug and "goodnight."

She always took it in stride. But in hindsight, I know she was disappointed that I never made a move. She was right. I was an idiot.

I SPENT the summer after my junior year of high school on Tybee Island working as a Lifeguard. The Blythe cousin who normally let us rent his place had a smaller place on the other side of the Island. He gave us free board in exchange for Paige and Kaitlynn working as waitresses at his wife's grill. I guess restaurants was a requisite of being a Blythe.

The days were hot and endless. They stretched as far and wide as the beach and sea. Tybee was a fun change of pace from Knox Ridge. There were still locals, sure. But every day brought new people from all over.

I met more people with interesting lives that summer than I had in the 17 years preceding it combined. Many of them were from around the South so it was easy to pick up a conversation with them.

My shift was in the morning, leaving most afternoons wide open to go exploring. I would slip into Savannah when I could or slip Kaitlynn out during her breaks. Regularly, I did both. We drove to

South Carolina every so often or walked the streets of Tybee every opportunity we had.

It was one of the best summers of my life because I didn't have to overthink anything. I got to drink in the world, sunshine, and spend it all with Kit Kat.

"We should buy a boat," she joked one afternoon as we floated rental paddle boards perpendicular to the shore.

"Yeah, why?"

"So we could take it sailing up and down the coast," I asked.

"No, to stop worrying about where we paddle out to or who we're renting from. Just have a floating hotel."

I grimaced. "What? Like that boat house the douchebag Kelsey dated last summer was building?"

She laughed as she leaned over to shove me. "There's nothing wrong with wanting more quality time on the water."

I shrugged. The world was so big back then, and in ways I could barely fathom. I wanted to conquer every inch, learn it by heart, and take what I could. I wanted to learn so much from the experience of living. But I never had the opportunities my peers had.

I couldn't go to sleepaway camp or travel for fun. The furthest I had been at that point was Arizona as a small child. Mom and I hadn't been further than Alabama since I was six. There was so much I hadn't seen yet and I was too stubborn and impatient to let anything get in my way.

"Why stop at the coast? Why not use a boat to go everywhere?" I asked.

"Like...sail around the world?"

"Sure," I said. "We could see everything out there. Make the world our bitch."

She shrugged with a weak smile.

"What?" I asked.

"...Traveling the world could take a while," she said. "It could even take years."

I looked out toward the horizon, smiling as I imagined all the places we could see.

"Maybe even decades," I said with a laugh.

"That's not funny," she said.

"It's exciting is what it is."

She frowned and pressed her lips so tight, her jaw tensed.

I sighed, disappointed by her lackluster response. "Seriously, Kit Kat, what's the big deal? The world is big. Everyone knows that."

"...That's a long time away from Knox Ridge," she said.

Who cares? I almost said. "So?"

"So...our entire lives are there," she said. "I'd miss everyone. Wouldn't you?"

I shrugged. "It's just a place."

She stood up on her board. She grabbed her paddle and started, well, paddling away.

"What are you doing?" I shouted.

"Running away from this stupid conversation," Kaitlynn said.

"What I'd say?"

She turned her board around enough to face me completely. Her eyebrows were raised in surprise. "Are you fucking kidding me?"

She sighed annoyed at me. Clearly, I didn't understand. "Knox Ridge isn't just a place, Oliver. It's not some accessory you can throw away the second you decide you're too old for it."

She didn't get it. She was too attached to Knox Ridge, this little home she'd always had. Knox Ridge was a given for her and she'd never had to contend with feeling like she belonged there.

She was a Blythe.

Knox Ridge was *made* for her. She didn't understand.

To me there was so much more beyond that town and so many

opportunities I felt were wasted on people who didn't appreciate it. I didn't understand until much later that I resented her for leaving me for Rhode Island the previous summer.

She had a level of freedom I had never known, and she chose it over *me*. Someday, I would grow up and realize how wrong it was to think that. But at seventeen, all I could wonder was how fast it would take her to leave me again.

And worse, would she even care if I left Knox Ridge?

Would she even notice?

"Yeah?" I said, feeling stung and ready to be cruel. "Maybe *you're* just too immature to realize that there's nothing there for us. You think you're going to grow up and be your parents? So what? Having your little perfect life figured out doesn't make you better than me."

In hindsight, I fully expected her to come back and beat the living shit out of me.

Instead, she screamed, "And being a cocky asshole doesn't make *you* better than *me*."

She paddled away and didn't talk to me for two days after that.

MOST OF THAT summer was a blur, but in the best way possible. It was so many good moments of coming into my own as a person and being with my best friend. Kelsey spent most of that summer in California at some sort of camp. She came home skinnier and with a bad bleach job. But her demeanor had been replaced with something calmer, albeit just as spiteful as she normally was.

She came down with all the parents the week before our senior year of high school. Her jaw dropped after she took one look at me.

"My, my," she said. "Little Ollie Tanner, you've grown."

I blushed awkwardly. I might have shot up another three inches while she was away.

"He's been swimming all summer, dipshit," Paige said behind her.

I gained a few pounds of muscle as well.

"Whatever," Kelsey said. "We should hang out sometime, Tanner...It's been a while."

"I guess?" I said.

Even with Kelsey slowly circling me like a shark and finally being reunited with the adults in my life after two months apart, I spent most of that week attached to Kaitlynn at the hip.

Being on that beach with her brought back so many memories.

Every grain of sand or ray of sun gave me déjà vu, echoes of lives and the kids we used to be. I felt the pulse of everything I'd been through up until this point in my life. Every single moment I could think of had Kaitlynn by my side, always there to help me fight my battles or carry my burdens.

This beach and vacation house felt like home because of how much of me was tied to this island and separating myself from the baggage of Knox Ridge. The world was calm here, almost perfect. Kaitlynn was a part of that.

She felt more like home to me than anything or anyone beyond my mother.

Kaitlyn was my firefly in a dark abyss, bathing everything she touched with her warmth.

I could have spent forever looking at her.

"What?" she asked shyly one afternoon when we were laying on the beach together and she caught me staring, again.

"Nothing," I said quietly, my mouth suddenly dry. "Just...enjoying the view."

WE GOT BACK to Knox Ridge day before my senior year of high school started. It was still summer, so the sun was high in the sky upon our arrival. We divided everything between the two households and unpacked everything in an orderly fashion.

Twelve summers of these trips had made me a pro in my post-Tybee rituals. Including heading out to my backyard, once I was done putting things away, to say goodbye to the summer.

That's where I would always find Kit Kat, standing on the other side of the fence, watching the sun slip behind the clouds. We mostly just talked about our days when we met like that. She'd normally ask what my favorite part of our trip was and what I'd miss the most.

This time was no different.

"The freedom," I said.

"You loved the freedom or you'll miss the freedom?"

"Both," I said solemnly. "I don't know if I'll ever be that person again."

Everything was changing. This was my last year of high school. One way or another, things would be different by the end of my senior year.

I expected her not to get it. She was always so confident and assured about her place in life. She was brave and straightforward where I was inconsistent, and almost spineless at times.

How could someone as perfect as her understand a mere mortal like me, I thought not long before that conversation.

"I know what you mean," she said quietly, staring at the sun. "It was so different out there. I wasn't Kaitlynn fucking Blythe, little miss sunshine picking up the slack for Kelsey Blythe. I was just another waitress in a vacation town who no one cared to give a second glance at. Hardly anyone remembered my name and they didn't care enough to recognize me if they did."

She swallowed thickly. "It was fucking beautiful...and it terrifies me to think I'm going to spend the rest of my life around people who think they know me better than I ever will. Just because they grew up with my dad or grandad or fucking Uncle Jim."

Her face looked so beautiful and glowing in the fading light, yet somehow older than her years. Kaitlynn hardly ever let her mask of dutiful daughter slip. But this was one of those rare moments where I could see the cracks. She understands what people expect of her, and then expects herself to execute it flawlessly.

I know being a Blythe is hard, I remember her mother telling me years before.

I wanted to tell her that no one who matters should expect so much of her. Or that her life is her own life. I think I even wanted to ask her to run away with me, start a new life somewhere where no one had ever heard of us. Take off the shackles of being a Tanner and Blythe, the descendants of the town drunks and the town founders.

I really wanted to tell her that someday she could just be Kaitlynn, I could be Ollie, and life could be whatever we felt like making it.

But my confidence shook as I thought all these things. What if it scared her off and she never left town? What if she laughed in my face for trying to defy destiny?

"Let's catch some fireflies," I said instead.

Chasing fireflies was one of our favorite past times. We had our strategy down to an art. It was all about meeting them where they were and gently ushering them into our jars. We never kept them too long, for fear of disrupting their way of life.

Each one had its own story that we'd tell each other as we released them. Most of them had families and friends to go back to, some just missed the taste of the wind in their wings. We threw so much of ourselves into those fireflies, sometimes we tangled fiction with our darkest secrets and our impressions of each other without a second thought.

It was hard to discern reality from the stories we told ... in hindsight that was on purpose.

Being vulnerable was hard.

Weaving a story with threads of truth and lying to ourselves that it made us feel heard was so much easier.

"This one doesn't really want to go home," Kaitlynn said one time. "But he doesn't think anyone will love him anywhere else."

I always wondered if it was her or me she was talking about.

Maybe it was both.

A week later, after coming back from work, I was tireless and went to the back yard. I accidentally ran into her, toppling both of us into the grass with me on top of her.

"Ow, geez, Ollie," she said, rubbing her head.

"Sorry," I said nervously. "Are you okay?"

I brushed away some hair from her face to get a better look. Her eyes were almost iridescent in the twilight.

Every inch of her was enchanting.

She was joy, she was grace...and she was home.

She was the most important person in the universe to me, especially with her lips two inches away from mine.

Her long eyelashes fluttered like they expected something to happen, like being swept away.

I remember how close her lips were as I bent down to finally do something...show her how much and how big I felt for her—

"Huey!" my mom yelled at the same time. "Curfew! Get your little tush onto bed."

—And I also remember the feeling of crippling remorse as I got up slowly, pulling away before I kissed Kaitlynn.

The shock on her face scared me so bad, I ran inside without saying goodbye. It was stupid and childish of me, but I saw myself *hurting* her—disappointing her in a way no one ever had before. I couldn't be responsible for that.

This was how I realized that I was in *love* with Kaitlynn Hope Blythe.

That was also how I realized that I couldn't jeopardize my relationship with her, or her family, by ruining my friendship with her. She was a Blythe; I was the descendant of the drunk Tanners. Everyone was waiting for me to pick up the liquor and start doing stupid shit around town.

What would the town do if I hurt her?

Fire my mom?

Kick us out of town?

Could I even survive without Kaitlynn in my life?

I was so terrified of losing her, I ran in the opposite direction.

FIVE

Kaitlynn

NANA USED to say that the stars were filled with wishes made by lonely hearts. Those days, I became one of those lonely hearts. Some nights, I walked around the dark backyard with a crowded head and an empty heart.

One night I felt his lips so close to mine. The warmth of his skin, the fire in his eyes. One second everything I've ever wanted was almost mine. The next he was gone. He vanished into the night and we were never the same again.

A few days later ...

It became official. It happened out of the blue. No one saw it coming. It slapped me on the face and shattered my heart into a billion pieces.

Everyone talked about it.

Oliver Tanner started dating my sister, Kelsey, at the beginning of their senior year of high school. At the time, the sight of them together made me want to puke. Not puke as in "they were so disgustingly sweet together I couldn't take it," but "they made no sense whatsoever and every time I saw the love of my life with my older sister, it was physically painful."

He was mine. I loved him first.

Yep, I was that naïve. Here, I had thought we were so close to getting together. I had felt his eyes on me the entire summer before that.

Was it all in my head?

Did I make up some fantasy about us being...in 'like' together that I deluded myself into thinking I had a chance with him?

Maybe I was or not, but I could never compare myself to Kelsey's beauty. Every guy in town wanted her—even my best friend.

Ollie and Kelsey were...something together. They were labeled as the *It-couple* in school. They were beautiful people who looked beautiful being together. They were the talk of the town and the envy of many.

People tried to keep the gossip away from me too much of no avail. I knew people were confused. I knew they were disappointed that Kelsey was the Blythe sister he was dating. I was too.

Maybe if they had been happy together, I could have gotten over my feelings for him. If I had truly felt like Kelsey could do right by him and he could do right by my sister, I think I would have had no choice but to accept their relationship and move on with my life.

I moved on...for the most part, but I never accepted them being together. They were passionate about each other in the kind of way that children were passionate about a new toy. They saw the surface of each other and never cared to dig deeper.

Kelsey dated the hottest guy in town. Guys finally accepted Oliver because he dated the girl every high school boy dreamed of having. No one saw what I did. A train wreck. The worse of all was their casualty. My heart.

Half the time they were so incredibly dissonant that their continued relationship made no sense. They had nothing in common except for work. He loved the outdoors and adventuring; she loved strategy games and makeup.

They didn't like the same shows or music. They were constantly arguing about everything because they were both too stubborn to ever accept defeat.

The year they dated in person was like watching a Mutual of Omaha's Wild Kingdom video of two bighorn sheep knocking heads over and over and *over* again. Sometimes it was more annoying to watch than it was painful because of how uncompromising they were.

One time, Kelsey and Ollie broke up for a week because they couldn't agree on some stupid concert and who the lead singer for Killing Hades was. Jacob Decker or some other dude I had never heard of. It's Kade Hades. I knew the answer, but I didn't care to tell them how stupid and pathetic they were.

They proceeded to spend that entire week playing telephone through me and constantly venting to Paige and me about why the other was so wrong.

That was the hell I lived in junior year of high school.

It crept by so slowly. I spent any extra time I could hiding out at Paige's house or hanging out with Josey or at the restaurant whenever the other two weren't around. Which, admittedly, was hard considering Kelsey was a hostess and Ollie was a waiter. But I found creative ways to keep my distance, as well as sanity, intact.

As if it weren't bad enough that half the school looked at me with pity, Ollie was pulling away harder than ever. He had talked over the summer about how Knox Ridge wasn't big enough for him and how he wanted a "fresh start."

So, I expected he wasn't going to stay in Georgia for college, but things got worse.

"The fucking Army?" I heard Kelsey scream in our kitchen one evening in late April. "Are you fucking kidding me?!"

"I told you I can't afford college!" Ollie said just as loud.

I was sitting on the back porch of our house. Nature watching was the best way I knew to calm me down back then. I did most of my thinking outside when I was younger.

"So, what do you expect? Am I supposed to be a happy little military wife, getting dragged all over the world because you're too stupid to take out some student loans?" she cried. "Un-fucking-believable."

"Because going to a fucking party school I can't afford is such a good idea?" he shouted back. "Admit it, Kelsey, you don't care what's best for me—you just want someone to follow you to college, so you won't be alone."

I winced. For once...I knew Kelsey was right. It was a big emotional toll to be an army wife. There were many women who did it and excelled amazingly. But Kelsey was barely eighteen. She didn't know what she wanted out of breakfast the next morning, much less life.

How could she possibly agree to a life that separated her from everyone and everything she'd ever known?

A life that might make her a young widow.

Ollie couldn't expect her to get on board with that when he was already halfway out the door and hadn't discussed it with her. Ollie, however, was also right.

Kelsey expected everyone to fall in line with her demands. She didn't compromise. She fought tooth and nail to get exactly her way.

It also made sense why he wanted to enlist. There were good benefits and he wouldn't have crippling student debt hanging over his head. It was a way to travel the world like he's always wanted without going bankrupt.

Yes, it was grueling, life-threatening work. But knowing Ollie, how ready he was to start somewhere new and how poor and useless this world had made him feel—I understood why he thought this was his only way out.

"Well excuse me for thinking that our relationship means anything to you," Kelsey said.

"Don't give me that bullshit," Ollie said. "There's nothing worth sticking around for in this shitty town and if you weren't so afraid of not being the prettiest girl in the room, you'd agree with me."

Ouch, I thought. *Nothing?*

I couldn't believe after all those years, we meant nothing to him. I swallowed back a few tears. I didn't mean anything to him and there was nothing I could do about it.

There was some rustling coming from the kitchen, they were probably making out angrily. They did that a lot in those days.

The last thing I heard before Ollie came storming out into the backyard was Kelsey shouting, "Don't expect me to be waiting around for you to get your head out of your ass! You hear me, Oliver Tanner? You're nothing without me."

I winced as Ollie slammed the door shut behind him. He groaned loudly. I looked up just as he was rubbing his temples harshly.

"You'll get wrinkles like that," I said.

"I'll live," he said bitterly as he sat next to me.

We sat in silence for a while. We used to be so comfortable with each other. But we'd become virtual strangers in less than a few months. I didn't know what to tell him.

If the right thing to do was confront him about how shitty he was being, or support someone who was clearly hurting and needed someone on their side.

Did he even care about my opinion? Probably not.

"My mom spent so many years saving," he said. "She took all those extra shifts. She took that second job...fuck, I had *multiple* jobs...We were supposed to be okay."

It was second nature. I could hear Nana say, "that boy needs some TLC."

I wrapped an arm around his shoulders. It barely worked because they were so broad at that point, but I did what I could. He was right, it fucking sucked. We grew up being told "work hard, good things will come your way."

Well they worked harder than anyone I've ever met and what happened?

All it took was one injury and Ollie's entire college fund was gone. Thank fuck their house had been in the family for years or else they might have lost that too. My parents gave as much as they could but running a restaurant and regularly feeding four kids added up.

That didn't include the money they spent on helping the rest of the town or saving so Kelsey and I could go to college.

"So, about what I said in there..." Ollie said eventually.

"Don't worry about it," I said. "You're right, nothing should hold you back from doing what you need to do."

He sighed, sagging into my side. Maybe that was the absolution he needed in order to leave. Regardless of if he ever cared about my opinion, maybe hearing poor little Katy Blythe—the girl doomed to live out her days in Knox Ridge—saying he could go was enough to let him.

He enlisted a week later.

OLIVER LEFT for Basic Training on a wet and stormy afternoon.

His mom would drive him over the night before. She planned to stay at a hotel before she dropped him off. My parents closed the restaurant for that day to see him off.

Mom cooked and we had lunch there. We spent more time than necessary lamenting about how great Ollie was and how much we were going to miss him. We took turns along with Paige's family, who took time off to see him as well, the restaurant staff, and some close family friends to tell stories about Ollie.

It bothered me at the time how much it felt like a wake for a person who wasn't dead yet. In hindsight, I think that was the point. They wanted an opportunity to remember Ollie while he was still a bright-eyed, naive kid. They knew that even if he came back alive, he'd never be the same person again.

We walked through the restaurant, pointing to things that had a specific memory to us or reminded us of Ollie. The adults kept telling him how proud they were of him and what a wonderful young man he was. Three years later, I would realize that they were giving him pep talks to carry with him. They wanted him to hear shit that could get him through the hard days.

I was too angry, sad, and oblivious to do the same.

The rain was still pounding hard outside when we parted with our friends and headed back to the Blythe and Tanner homes. Paige rode in the backseat of my parent's car with me while Ollie and Kelsey went with Josey. I hugged the life out of Paige. We might've grown apart, but it felt as if I was losing one best friend that day. Guess I didn't want to lose her either.

We stood on the front porch of my house, watching the rain solemnly.

"If Nana were here she'd say we're idiots for being on the porch. We should either stay warm inside or wash our tears out in the fucking rain," Paige said.

Dad laughed. "She sure would."

Mom squeezed Ollie's shoulder behind him. "She loved you so much, Ollie. I know if she were here, first she'd tell you 'don't die of stupid.' Then she'd hug you really tight and tell you the Blythe family motto."

Ollie nodded. "Keep fighting, keep loving," he recited.

"Keep the faith and get home safe," I finished it with a trembling voice.

Ollie turned around and gave my mom the biggest hug I'd ever seen. I never forgot how much love he poured into a single hug. To this day, I swear I saw a few tears sting his eyes.

"Bye, honey," Mom said. "We'll see you soon, okay?"

Ollie went to give my dad a handshake but was pulled into a hug instead.

"Don't let that big bad world shake you around too hard, son," Dad said.

Ollie mumbled something that made Dad hug him harder.

Years later, Ollie would tell me he'd whispered, "I won't, Dad."

Paige practically tackled him in a hug. "You're a pain in the ass," she said through tears. "And you smell really bad—But if you die, I will drag you back from Hades and kill you again myself."

Ollie laughed. "I'll miss you too, squirt."

He and Kelsey kissed for a bit. The way she said, "goodbye, Tanner," quietly, is the only proof I have that she ever cared for him. It was the most vulnerable I had seen her since Nana's death and would be the only time for many years to come.

The rain let up as they exchanged goodbyes. The sky was overcast but calm for the first time in days.

"We should get rolling before the rain starts up again," Josey said. "Heaven knows there's nothing I hate more than drivers who don't know how to drive in the rain."

Ollie nodded, clearing his throat. He looked at me expectantly and tilted his head toward the car.

"I'll walk you," I offered.

It wasn't more than a hundred feet to Josey's car, but it was the longest walk of my life. So much had happened in the last thirteen years of our lives together. I couldn't remember what my life was without Oliver.

He was quiet fall afternoon, exciting days at the beach, late-night movie marathons, and the wide-open sky. He was everything that made Knox Ridge special, wrapped into one person. It felt like a part of me was dying with him.

We would never be these kids again, even if we survived long enough to meet again.

Would we ever meet again?

He hugged me tight. Tighter than he hugged Mom and longer than he kissed Kelsey. I held onto him praying for his safety and wanting for him to stay with me.

"Keep chasing fireflies," he mumbled.

"I'll write you," I said. Because I couldn't stand to hear myself say goodbye.

"That would be great," he said quietly.

It sounded off and to get him off the hook I said, "You, uh, don't have to write me back."

"I will," he said earnestly. "As much as possible."

When we got to Josey's car, he turned around to face me. He shrugged as if to say "well...that's it."

I almost opened my mouth to ask if he really had to leave. But I realized how selfish it would be if I did. Whether he wanted to admit it or not, Knox Ridge was a part of him. He was leaving the only home he ever knew. I could see the trepidation in his eyes. He was just as scared as I was.

Instead, I hugged him tightly for one last time.

"Goodluck, Ollie-pop," I whispered.

"Won't need luck, Kit Kat," he whispered back.

I watched and waved as his mom drove him away. The rain returned soon after their departure, shrouding the world and me in a blanket of dense, cold rain. Somehow, the rain felt warmer than my heart.

I wouldn't see Oliver Tanner again for twelve years.

Chapter Six

TWELVE YEARS ago

OLLIE,

I'm praying for your safety. Let me know if you need anything else.

Love,

Kaitlynn

P.S. Share the goodies with your friends.

KIT KAT,

Thank you for taking the time to mail me so many wonderful things. I put most of them to good use and shared them as well. Receiving this made my day. It reminded me of home. Thank you for your prayers.

God bless,

Oliver
P.S. How's everything at home?

OLLIE,

Home is ...nothing has changed. My parents had gotten a little more ridiculous than usual. They considered themselves empty-nesters. Paige and I are next. We caught them making out in the employee's room at the restaurant.

We consider the house a non-safe zone because what if we catch them having sex in the kitchen—ewww.

You're welcome for the mental image. It's been haunting me ever since I found Mom and Dad making out in the kitchen.

I have nightmares!

Did you hear that your mom met some guy?

He's handsome. Well, handsome for his age. What we know: Toby is some rich guy from Montgomery, Alabama. He owns dealer-ships in the state and Arkansas. He's super sweet with Josey. At least, that's what we've seen so far.

My parent's like him. We all like him. We hope this is it because she deserves someone to love her and take care of her.

Next time let me know what you'd like from home. After every-thing that you're doing for our country, the least I should do is keep you happy—or at least try. Sorry if I sound selfish or insensitive. I'm trying not to be either. Writing you is kind of hard because I have no idea what you're going through.

Every time I watch the news, I'm terrified for our troops—and you. It makes me want to fly to Afghanistan and bring you home. I'd love to hear more about you, how things are going—within reason.

Let me catch you up on my life. I'm off to Los Angeles. UCLA accepted me.

Can you believe it?

I'm going to be pursuing a media and television degree. My parents aren't happy about it since my sister moved to New York. (I heard that you guys broke up. I'm sorry. She sucks but I want you to know this doesn't change anything between the two of us.)

My parents are unhappy because they don't have anyone to boss around at their restaurant. But it is what it is, you know? My dreams don't include staying in Knox Ridge, tending to the family restaurant.

Please, don't get me wrong, I love Blythe's and my parents. Well...love the parents and like Blythe's. But if I want to host my own cooking show, I have to find my own way. Just like you did. I admire and respect how you took charge of your life and knew all along what you wanted to do.

Be safe.

Love,

Kaitlynn

KIT KAT,

Your package and letter not only brightened my day, but I'm relieved to know that I'm not losing my best friend after what happened with Kelsey. Actually, I have no fucking idea what happened with your sister.

Do you?

Her last email only said that we were over, and that was the end of it. I can't wrap my head around it. Who am I kidding, we barely emailed each other since I left Knox Ridge. Still a phone call would've been nice.

Things around here are fucking insane. We have to watch our backs every second. Your packages and letters are the highlights of my day. Please keep sending them. Things are too dark here and receiving a little sunshine from you makes it bearable.

Good luck in LA.

OT

TEN YEARS ago

Ollie,

Please accept this care package. It traveled from Knox Ridge to Los Angeles. Mom gathered some things from home. I know how much you like to have a taste of the south when possible. Though, I packed the moonpies well so they make it to you in one piece, I can't guarantee it'll happen.

How are you doing?

I'm doing well. LA is worlds apart from our small town. The best thing is that I don't have to be worrying about the neighbors— or the town—tattle telling on me. No one cares about me. That's also the downside.

At home everyone cares for each other. School has handed me my behind several times, but I'm still standing.

Sorry for the short letter but I need to study for finals. Keep your fingers crossed, I applied for an internship. I need a job. More like an excuse not to go home.

Be safe.

Love,

Kaitlynn.

NINE YEARS AGO,

Kit Kat,

Thank you for the books you sent over. I shipped them to Afghanistan. At the moment, I'm stationed in The United Kingdom. I'm learning new things, going to school and hoping that the war ends soon. Though, it doesn't look like that's ever going to happen.

How is school?

Are you still working at that French restaurant? To be fair, I'm sending you a few goodies from this country. Hope to hear from you soon.

OT

EIGHT YEARS ago

Ollie,

I heard from Mom that you're going back to the frontlines. Please stay safe.

Love,

Kaitlynn.

OLIVER,

It's good to hear from you. Congratulations on the new rank. A lot has changed in my life too. I have a new boyfriend. His name is Steve. He's charming, and a great comedian. Hope you're doing well.

Your friend,

Kaitlynn

SIX YEARS ago

Ollie,

How are you, soldier? Long time not talking to you.

I hope the cookies made it in one piece, along with everything else. Let me know what you think of them. If everything goes as planned, I might start marketing them. There's so much I have to tell you, but the SparkNotes are as follows:

1)   Kelsey finally graduated. She's a teacher—who knew she'd want to shape young minds.

2)   I got a job in Atlanta—the Food Network hired me!

3)   I moved out of LA.

4)   I broke up with Esteban—my first long-term relationship. *insert a broken heart*

Now you're caught up with my life. There's more, but let's save the drama for later. When you come back home, we can share a meal and talk.

When are you coming back?

Love,

Kaitlynn

KAITLYNN,

I was beginning to wonder about your whereabouts. It's been a long time since I've heard from you. The cookies were incredible. Send as many as you want. I'll be happy to taste test them for you. The next time I'm in the US, I promise I'll contact you. Your Spark-Notes are too condensed to understand what's really going on with your life.

What happened to those long letters you used to send?

I miss them, along with the little drawings you'd make next to your notes. In any case, let me respond to your comments.

1)   I'd rather not comment on your sister.

2)   *Congratulations on the new job, and I wish I were home to help you move.*

3)   *Sorry about LA. I know you loved living there.*

4)   *I'm sure this guy was a loser, glad you are done with him.*

OT

OLLIE,

I remember having more time to write to you back in college than I have now. Adulting isn't easy. You can't judge Esteban. You never met the man. I have to confess that I liked him better when he was just Steve. Who changes his name to be a standup comedian?

Good riddance.

When you say the next time I visit the US, you sound as if you've been here to visit and never notified me.

I confess that I'm a little hurt. Let me know how the new batch of cookies tastes.

Love,

Kaitlynn

OLIVER,

I forgot to mention during our call that Cynthia and Richard passed away. I know you're on a mission and can't reach me but call me when you can.

Love,

Mom

SEVEN

Kaitlynn

Five Years Ago

It was the middle of the night when I received the call.

"Just so you know, Mom and Dad were in a car accident. The sheriff says they died at the scene. Since you're closer, you should drive down there. I won't be able to fly home until Monday."

Kelsey didn't wait for me to say anything. She just hung up and left me crying and trembling with the news. I called Paige right away. She was already at the sheriff's office; her dad was coming home to help her until I came home.

Stupid Kelsey came home when I had everything under control. She demanded I cancel the arrangements because she wanted "a quiet affair" to say goodbye to our parents. It's like she wanted them buried in the dead of night so that no one could see them.

I have no clue what she was thinking. Instead of giving them the large reception they deserved, the entire town would be crammed into our house to view their caskets.

Not that I let her. I arranged the best funeral I could on such short notice. Everyone and their relatives passed through our house every night that February. They dropped food saying, "it's not as good as your parent's but we made it with love."

They were gone and I couldn't understand what happened. I had just spoken with them earlier that day about my show and tried to convince Mom to give away a few of our family recipes.

"Over my dead body, Kaitlynn Hope Blythe. Nana would kill me if I let you share them with the world. They are Blythe recipes."

I promised never to share them, and I told her how much I missed her. Before we said goodbye, Mom and Dad promised to drive to Atlanta to visit me. That'd never happen.

The officer on duty said they hydroplaned into the intersection on a red light. The truck that ran into them didn't have time to stop. The coroner said they both had severe neck and spine trauma. Paige said they had been on there way back from a furniture store when it started to rain.

After the funeral, Kelsey ordered me to stop crying.

That's all she said to me for a week straight.

The next time Kelsey spoke to me, it was to say she was selling our parents' house.

"Are you kidding me?" I said angrily. "They're not even cold in the ground and—fuck who would even buy this place? It's the Blythe house."

Kelsey shrugged, her frown was detached, and her stance was frigid. Her eyes were listless, like she had died with them.

"Don't be so dramatic. A couple moving into town wanted to buy it," she said quietly. "They made a good offer. It'll be a good rainy-day fund until I figure out what to do with the restaurant."

My body went cold, as frozen and lifeless as the last time I'd seen our parents. Something snapped in me. I wanted to scream or fight her. I felt trapped in my own body, like I was being held down as a hostage in my own life.

"How are you okay with this? Some strangers are going to take over everything we've ever cared about—"

"What do you want me to say, Katy?" Kelsey shouted. "I'll just keep the house as it collects dust? Do you think I should stay in Knox Ridge until some jackass like Sheldon Stern or Carl Mulligan decide it's time to get married and pick me to 'court?' I should give up my entire fucking life to play house while Mom and Dad are out? Newsflash, they're never coming back!"

I shift nervously, averting my eyes from her. "That's not what I'm saying—"

"Oh good, thanks your majesty," Kelsey said. Then she sighed. "It's my house. They gave it to me. Their first born...I can't look at it anymore. So, you can either make a better offer than the one this family gave me, or you can shut up and help pack everything up."

I nodded.

She put a hand on my shoulder, squeezing once like Mom used to, before she trudged toward the kitchen.

Something about us broke that day. She blamed me for something I didn't do ... and I think to some extent I blamed her too. For not being able to fill the void of our parents, not taking their death well, or maybe just for selling my childhood home. We didn't know how to talk to each other after their death.

I never recovered from that.

JOSEY TANNER LEFT Knox Ridge five years ago. She got married to a man from her hometown in Alabama who ran into her on Tybee the year before. She said they were friends while growing up but lost track when she married Oliver's dad.

We were happy for her and up until my parent's died, she split her time between Knox Ridge and Alabama. That's how it went for a few years, my parents and I would tend to the house while she was out, and she always brought the best presents in return.

She didn't make it to the wake, but Josey made it to my parents' burial. She had to be. She hugged me tightly. I think she's the only reason I got through that week. We spent a lot of time on her couch, watching movies like we used to in high school. Paige joined us every night. This time it came with a bottle of wine, more blankets, and a somber cloud over all of us.

Kelsey barely packed shit when it was time to move all our parents earthly belongings out of our childhood home. Paige and Josey helped with that too. Every so often we'd pick up something that, for whatever reason, sparked a memory of my parents. It took us an entire afternoon to get through the photo albums and books...and another to get through their bedroom.

The hardest ordeal was working through the kitchen. Everything in there was touched by their love, their essence. There wasn't a single dry eye when we started in on it.

After a futile attempt to get through tossing everything in the fridge, Josey dried her eyes.

"You know, it seems like a shame that all this food is getting tossed," she said. "I think it would make your parents happy if we used this kitchen one last time."

That's how we spent an afternoon making too many sweets and the oddest everything-casserole I would ever eat. It was delicious though, a strange hodge podge of ingredients but they all worked harmoniously.

Just like Knox Ridge.

Just like my parents had been.

"So I was thinking," Josey said while we ate that casserole. "It's getting hard to make it over here every couple of months so...this might be my last trip for a while."

Paige and I frowned at each other. "But Josey," I started to protest.

"Honey, it's alright, y'all can visit me whenever you're out my way," she said. "I'll still be around but...I think it's time for a new chapter for old Josey."

I laughed in spite of everything. She was barely forty-five and she knew it.

"What about your house?" Paige asked.

Josey took a deep breath. "I think it's time to pass it down to Oliver. This was always meant to be his. You can bring some of these boxes to the garage, Kaitlynn."

My stomach dropped. Great, the fate of this place I grew up in is in the hands of someone who hasn't stepped foot in this town in years. Someone who hated this town. He probably didn't care about us anymore.

How could he?

Knox Ridge was so special from the inside, but I know what people saw outside looking in. They saw nothing, a drive by town at best and a backwater waste of space at worst. I knew that's how sick he was of us at the end...and of me. He had seen the world. The beautiful things and the horrible too. He was a man of the world. No longer the boy who grew up in a small town.

How was I supposed to trust someone who was virtually a stranger with something so precious to me?

"But in the meantime," Josey said with a quirk of her lips. "I think it's alright if I entrust it to some wonderful young women I know for safe keeping."

I smiled through ugly tears.

We hugged her tightly for far too long that day. For a moment, the world didn't feel so big and terrible.

WEEKS WENT BY, and then months. The dust settled and Knox Ridge slowly started to move on from the wake of Richard and Cynthia Blythe's untimely deaths. Kelsey took over the restaurant and Paige went back to work.

I did what my parents expected when I moved to Atlanta and drove every weekend to Knox Ridge.

The town started chugging again, just like it always did when the time for mourning was "over." I never understood how other people could tell when it was time to move on, but I wasn't there yet.

I wasn't even close.

Paige and her parents took me to Tybee that year. We rented the same house we always did. My uncle handed over the key with an awkward pat. I waited until we got inside to break down crying. The beach and water were as beautiful as ever, at least that's how it looked from Paige's photos years later.

I spent most of that trip either sitting on the beach staring out into the ocean or wading around the breakers staring at the horizon. I stared at the vastness of the ocean, feeling nothing but loneliness.

I tried to move on that autumn, thinking enough time had passed that I should have been over it by then. I was wrong.

Sometimes I'd bury myself in work for weeks on end. Sometimes I'd spend hours staring at the walls of my apartment in Atlanta. I wrote Ollie letters that were never answered. At first, I wondered if he even wanted to talk to me. Then I stopped caring and stopped mailing them.

I spent most of Thanksgiving and Christmases holed up in the Tanner house, curled in a ball on the couch as the TV flickered in front of me. The world forgot about the Blythes, about me, and I forgot about the world.

Paige checked on me when she could but she had her own life.

The days blurred and work became my only priority. I came

down to Knox Ridge when I could. I thought if I stayed around long enough, I could find a way to say goodbye to my parents properly. As if maybe there was an answer to this tragedy that I could find biking through the streets or fixing Ollie's car.

All I found, however, was loneliness and despair everywhere I looked.

That's how it would be for many years to come.

... After
_____

EIGHT

Oliver

AT EIGHTEEN, I had no clue what I wanted to be. My mother encouraged me to go to college, but even if I wanted to, we couldn't afford it.

I grew up in a place where there weren't many chances to become someone. At least, not for a guy without a college degree and a single mother who struggled her entire life. I figured that joining the army was my only viable option—my free ticket out of the despair that waited for me.

The military life offered me more than staying behind to work as a construction worker, or a waiter, like my mother. Joining the army was a no-brainer. They had financial aid, free healthcare, and job security. Those weren't my only motivators, but they were the strongest.

By becoming a soldier, I could serve my country and prove that I could be a part of something bigger than myself. During my twelve years of service, I got all these benefits, financial and more.

I made lifelong friends, achieved an education, and fulfilled a career. I also learned to appreciate the simple things in life.

Twelve years later, however, I retired without a plan.

Leaving the army wasn't the end of the world, but I still can't seem to find my place. So, I'm a civilian. Big deal. I'm no longer "Captain Oliver H. Tanner." Just Oliver Hugh Tanner, a man who only has military qualifications, an unused business degree, and is *fucking lost* in the Georgia heat.

My personal hurricane is about to start.

As I walk off of the plane, I feel the high temperature reflecting off the tarmac. It's as hard to breathe here as it was in Iraq. For a second, I'm back in a half-buried tent in the desert, fearing for my life.

The dense air smells like diesel. I'm sweating before I even reach the bottom of the steps. It's not just the heat or the godforsaken humidity—it's the people. I can feel it. The panic begins like a cluster of sparks in my abdomen. Tension grows in my face and limbs while my mind replays the last mission. My chest feels too fucking tight.

The air-conditioning at the gate offers no relief. I'm trapped in a large shed covered with glass as I scan the area for my ride out of here.

Where the fuck are you, Striker Frimston?

"Hey, Tanner!" A loud voice and a pat on my back draw me back into reality.

"Frimston," I found him, a full mop of dark blonde hair, towering above the crowd.

I relax only for a few seconds, but I still have to get out of this place.

"Are you okay, Cap?" He shakes my hand, giving me a brotherly hug.

"Let's get the hell out of here," I say. "The heat is killing me."

We walk through the hallways of the airport. My breathing

comes easier once we're away from the sea of people. The flight wasn't an issue.

What was it about the arrival that made me anxious?

My mind isn't what it used to be. As we reach the parking lot, Striker opens the trunk of a black Suburban. I put my backpack in and walk toward the passenger door.

"I don't remember Knox Ridge being this hot," I complain, taking off my jacket and climbing into the truck.

"When was the last time you visited?" Striker asks.

"More than a decade ago," I recall.

Between deployments and my mother moving back to Alabama, I haven't been in Georgia since the end of basic training. I haven't been here for longer.

"That long?" He whistles. "Your mom must miss you."

"I've seen her. She got married a couple of years after my first deployment, and as I said, she moved to Montgomery," I explain.

"How's that going?"

"Toby's alright. He treats her like a queen and swears it was love at first sight. Mom moved in with him without hesitation."

He nods with a stupid grin. "Love will make you change your entire life."

"I guess for some it works that way." I look out the window. "...How's Kaitlynn?"

"Blythe?"

"No, Kaitlyn Monroe, the veterinarian," I say sarcastically.

"Ah, well," he says. "It's Kaitlynn so...crabby as ever."

"Really?" I ask. Kaitlynn was always such a happy person.

He shrugs. "You know how it is, Tanner. She hasn't been the same since her parents died...None of the Blythe girls have been the same since then. Not even fucking Paige Williams, the honorary Blythe, is back in one piece."

Fuck, how much have I missed while I was away?

"Thank you for the lift. I appreciate it."

Striker's the greatest friend a guy could ask for. He's a couple of years older than me. We didn't cross paths until we were away from home. I met him during my first tour in Iraq. We quickly went from bunkmates to brothers, but what truly bonds us is Knox Ridge. It's not just a town, it's a part of who we are that we both gave up in order to seek out a different life.

"It's the least I could do. Plus, I want to run a couple of things by you. What are your plans?" Striker asks as he takes the highway toward downtown.

"I have no idea," I say honestly. "Mom left me her house to do whatever I want with it. That's why I decided to move here...for now."

"Any job prospects yet?"

I scratch the back of my neck, shrugging. "A couple. One of them entails going back to Iraq to do private security, but I'm not interested."

As Striker's car speeds past the sidewalks and houses, I admire the old Knox Ridge oak trees, steady and grounded. It's been so long since I've stepped foot in this town, some of it seems like a fractured memory at this point. I wonder if I'm ready to bury the ghosts of my childhood and let them lie.

I didn't leave Knox Ridge with the kindest feelings.

Have I really moved on?

"I'm in no hurry, but I don't think I'll be able to sit on my ass for long," I say.

"If you want something to keep you busy, HIB securities wants to build a team down here. Still State-side, of course, but with easier access to Miami and the Caribbean."

I huff. "Are you offering me a job?"

"Not me, but they can always use a guy like you, Tanner. Put your training to work, and at the same time help ease you back into civilian life."

"How hard was it for you?" I ask.

"It wasn't as hard as I imagined, but it took me some time to adapt. A couple of the owners are former Rangers. They helped me through more shit than you can imagine."

"I'll think about it," I say, absently as I look at my old childhood home.

The house is desperately in need of improvements. The dingy brick walls are drenched in dried up sludge from the leaky tin gutter that ran along the outer edge of the crumbling roof.

The bricks belong to another era, they're not a solid red, but swirled with hues of muted brown and sickly pink, giving the two-story dwelling a blotchy look.

I groan opening the passenger door. "I guess there's a lot to be done in this house too."

"If you need a place to stay, I have enough room," Striker offers.

"Thank you, man, but this is a palace compared to some of the places I've stayed in."

"Fair enough," he says with a chuckle. "Still, text me if you decide to take me up on the offer, or if you need anything."

"I will, Frimston." I shake his hand, shut the car door, and pick up my backpack from the trunk.

THIS HOUSE IS A MAUSOLEUM. Everything is original, like the house itself. The floral wallpaper has a yellow undertone. The furniture is sparse and simple. In the foyer sits a gray rotary telephone, with its large dialing disk and curled cable dangling from the receiver. It's been there since my grandparents lived here.

Mom said I could either renovate or just sell. If I did the

latter, the new owner would likely tear it down and build something new. Somehow, the idea of someone else living in this house, didn't sit well in the pit of my stomach. This house has a history. Every inch of it witnessed the lives of the Tanners.

I couldn't stomach to lose it the way the Blythe's lost their place. My stomach drops and my chest tightens. Richard and Nana come to mind. They loved the house. The history it gathered. How is it possible that they let it go?

Mom said it had been Kelsey. It doesn't surprise me. She never cared about anyone but herself. That's what made it so easy to be with her. I didn't have to think of anyone else but me. She made the last months in town bearable. Between parties and frivolous trips, I didn't have to think much about my life or what I'd leave behind if I decided to enlist.

My room is exactly how I left it. A picture of the Blythe sisters lays on top of the bookcase. I study it, pushing the bitter taste away. Mom once told me you can't love two people at the same time. She's right. I only loved one. I just was too much of a coward to accept it.

Kelsey poses for the camera like a professional model. Her long, brown hair cascading down her shoulders. Her bright smile is wide and as brilliant as her expressive eyes.

Next to her is little Kaitlynn, my best friend. Looking as beautiful as I remember. She's eating ice cream in the photograph, unaware that I was taking a picture of them.

That's Kit Kat in a nutshell—a little oblivious to her surroundings whenever there's food around, especially ice cream. As I recall the amount of sweets we used to eat together, my stomach grumbles.

Thankfully, my old 1969 Mustang is still in the garage. I pick up the keys from the hook where Mom left them and open the garage door, praying it'll start. I slide in the driver's seat, turn on the engine and push the gas pedal twice.

It purrs the same way it used to. I should be grateful it's even running. There's no way it should sound this healthy considering it hasn't been used in the last decade.

I drive toward the grocery store. But instead of turning left, I continue onto Main Street and search for a parking spot close to Blythe's.

The outside of the restaurant is as opulent as ever. The manor that houses it has a majestic exterior that features broad columned beams that soar upward, reaching beyond the double stacked front porches to frame the home beautifully. A walk-up front entrance boasts a brick exterior staircase. Nothing has changed, not even the open sign.

Mom worked here for as long as I can remember. The Blythes were always good to us, every single one of them from Nana all the way down to Kaitlynn.

I should check on her. It's been so long since she contacted me. I can't remember when I received her last letter. It's been even longer since I last saw her. I lock my car, walking toward the entrance. I come to a complete stop when I see Kelsey.

She's the last person I want to see—ever. Her tall frame and slender body are impeccable. Her blue eyes, like the midnight sea, are still and emotionless. Wavy blonde hair cascades smoothly down her back. The man next to her is tall and blond too, but not quite up to my six foot two.

"Oliver," she gasps, her hand touching her sternum. "This is a big surprise."

I nod. "Kelsey."

"John, this is Oliver," she says to the man. "An old family friend."

I snort. "Yes, family friend."

"He and his mother worked for us," she says.

"Oliver Tanner, ex-boyfriend and next-door neighbor," I introduce myself, offering a handshake.

"John Meeks, Kelsey's husband," he replies, shaking my hand with a firm grasp.

I glance at both of them. Husband? Who knew someone would put up with a high maintenance bitch like her? The day I told her I was going to enlist, she protested because she wouldn't be an army wife. After our fight, I mumbled. I wouldn't want you as my wife even if I didn't enlist.

Our relationship was just attraction. She used me as much as I used her. Her parents trusted me and didn't care about setting a curfew. They knew Mom had me under a tight leash.

John's phone rings. He sighs, and glances at Kelsey.

"It won't take me long, babe," he promises, walking away.

"Look, John and I have to drive up to Atlanta. I'm glad you're ..." She looks at me from head to toe, "... *alive*, but I don't see the point of this conversation."

She turns around and walks toward her husband. She waves her hand. "Have a good fucking life."

Kelsey hasn't changed. She's still the same selfish bitch I grew up with. She takes and takes until there's nothing left, then she jumps ship, leaving the rest of us to clean up after her messes. I should've never paid attention to her.

But she caught me at a vulnerable moment, when I had come to realize that what Kaitlynn and I had was fragile and I could break it just by being Oliver Tanner. Not that it's an excuse, just a fact of my stupidity when I was a teenager.

Back then this place was asphyxiating me. I ran so hard and so far from Knox Ridge without a second glance. I think I was relieved when Mom said she was moving back to Alabama. This town has too much history and I don't think I want to relive it.

Then, why am I back?

I look at my car and then back at the restaurant, debating what I should do next. It only takes me a few seconds to decide that I need to eat something. When I enter Blythe's, it's like coming home.

The large dining room windows frame the pleasant view of the garden. The greenery outside meshes well with the interior wooden walls to match the color palette of the landscape.

Everything is just slightly turned on its axis—familiar but different enough that the entire place is a new world, its own alternate universe.

The white walls are now yellow. The dining room seems smaller than I remember, somehow. As I turn toward the kitchen, everything around me stops.

A woman marches out of the kitchen. Her warm chestnut colored hair makes her beautiful pink lips stand out. Her cheeks are rough and chapped. She wears a grey t-shirt with *Blythe's* logo on it, and a pair of tight jeans.

I'm caught off guard by the confident, sexy strut that tells the world, *I'm in charge, move aside.* Her hair is pulled back into a ponytail. Her green eyes shine like twin emeralds, illuminating the grand dining hall.

As her gaze finds mine, I finally recognize her. Kaitlynn. I hold my breath when she smiles at me.

NINE

Oliver

_____

"OLLIE?" Kaitlynn says slowly, studying me from head to toe. "Oliver Hugh Tanner?"

I am unable to peel my gaze off her. The last time I saw Kaitlynn, was from the back of my mom's car as she drove me to Basic Training. She stood in front of our houses and waved me goodbye in the bitter rain. That was twelve years ago.

My heart shattered that night when I had to leave her behind. We've been so close for so long, and even though my senior year we barely spoke, she was there. I wanted to beg Mom to stop the car. For Kaitlynn to come with me. And finally, after all those years, she's here.

"Kit Kat," I say quietly, barely finding my voice.

"Oh, my God. It is you." She squeals and runs toward me, flinging her arms around my neck.

"It's been years." My heart pounds hard as I lift her, pressing her close to me.

This feels like a welcome home. I've never felt this kind of peace. After so many years of being away, I'm finally home.

Kaitlynn buries her face in the crook of my neck. I feel her warm breath caressing my skin. That smile, her voice, and her beautiful body all summon forth a well of emotion inside me.

Whoa. I release her, taking a step back.

What's going on?

I feel it, an imaginary thread pulling me toward her. Some force tugging me with an extraordinary power. As if she's capturing not only my attention, but my soul.

All my attention is hers, and I can't tame the instant arousal. It's like fire cascading through my body. There's static crackling around us, and electricity flowing through my chest.

What happened to you?

I stare at her beautiful face trying to comprehend who I'm looking at. This woman can't be the girl I've been corresponding with via mail for over a decade.

"A sack of flour exploded on my face?" She touches her dusty hair. "But why are you mumbling?"

"Sorry, I ..." I had nothing smart to say.

She glances at me, her green eyes studying me close. Her soft, small hands touching my jaw.

"I'm so glad you're here, Ollie. I thought I'd never see you again." She glances around the restaurant. "With your mom gone, I honestly thought that you were done with Knox Ridge."

"It's been so long since the last time I saw you," I say, unable to take my eyes away from her hypnotic gaze.

"I've missed you so much. Nothing's been the same since you left." She blows air moving some of the strands gracing her face. "You hungry?"

"As a matter of fact, that's why I'm here."

She claps with excitement. "What are you in the mood for? Wait...I know what you'd like."

"Do you now?" I sweep my eyes over her body and wink.

Her lips press together as her gaze narrows. Kaitlynn opens her mouth only to snap it shut right away.

"Yes, I do." She nods once.

Kaitlynn scans the restaurant and points at the empty booth in the southwest corner. "Take a seat. Let me place the order and bring you some crab cakes." She leaves, swaying her hips and leaving me stoic. I'm numbed by her beauty.

A server comes by with a glass of sweet tea and a plate of crab cakes as promised. "Miss Blythe will be by in a few minutes," he says.

Fifteen minutes later, she's back with a full tray of dishes. Tomato bisque, seafood pasta, seed crusted grouper, and fried chicken. I stare at the platters for several seconds. That's too much food, even for me.

"These look delicious but—"

"Shush," she says, taking a seat and setting one of the cups of soup in front of me. "I haven't had lunch either. We'll share a little of everything. Now, tell me what's going on with you. How long are you planning to stay in town?"

"I'm not sure." I grab a clean plate and serve myself a little of everything. "Mom's husband offered me a job."

"Selling cars?" She furrows her eyebrows. "I can't see you doing that."

Me neither.

"Striker Frimston offered me a job too," I blow out some air.

She huffs. "With that little 'secret' service company." She rolls her eyes while drawing quotations in the air. "They are okay, I think. And that sounds more like something you'd want to do. But you don't sound too sure about it either."

As she says that, my body relaxes, and so does my mind. She

might have blossomed from a kid into an attractive grown woman, but she's still my friend.

Fuck. I can't stop staring. She's so fucking hot.

"When I decided to retire, I didn't think about what I'd be doing. Now that I'm actually here...it's too real."

Kaitlynn reaches for my hand, squeezing it lightly. The gesture is innocent, though her touch sends a spark that travels through my body, zapping my groin. Fuck. In an instant, my dick's as hard as granite.

"You'll need time to adjust," she says, oblivious to how much she's affecting me.

"This is good." I take a bite of the pasta and snatch my hand away from hers, grabbing my glass and quenching my thirst with her sweet tea.

Nothing works. I'm still burning for her.

"Enough about me, what are you doing here?"

"Working?" She scrunches her nose, looks around the restaurant and sighs.

"Come on, Kit Kat. I need more than that."

"Kit Kat," she says, grimacing. "No one's called me that since Dad died."

She sits there, eyes downcast and face grief stricken. I reach for her hand, squeezing it carefully.

"I'm sorry about your parents," I say. *Should I ask what happened?*

My mom was never direct about how they died. Just that they did, and it was tragic.

"Thank you," she says.

She looks up. The spark in her green eyes is gone. All that's left is a faint trace of where her vibrant soul once lay. A few tears slip down her rosy cheeks. I pull an old handkerchief out of my pocket, handing it to her.

"Sorry," she says with a weak laugh. "I guess I still miss them."

Glancing around the restaurant, my chest feels heavy. The Blythes were good people. They always gave as much as they could, and their daughters were their pride and joy.

"They would hate to see me crying like this." She wipes her face furiously with the handkerchief. "Let's talk about something else."

"Tell me what's going on with you," I offer tentatively. "The last time I heard from you, you were living in Atlanta."

She stares at the ceiling. "When I was a producer for that show?"

"No, Mom mentioned that you had a job offer to work for the Food Network as a chef. What happened?"

She looks around the restaurant. "*Blythe's* happened."

"Because of your parents?"

"Well, Kelsey took over the restaurant at first. But then she wanted to sell it—just like she sold our childhood home." She looks around the Victorian home and says, "The house has been in the family for generations and she wanted to give it to some suit from New York with a five-dollar haircut and a six thousand-dollar tie."

"I can't imagine anyone else taking this place over," I say, instantly regretting it.

I'm the one who told her to move on from Knox Ridge. I'm the one who goaded her into getting a different life.

She nods, stabbing the food on her plate with a fork. "I couldn't let her. This was my parents' dream. Their *legacy*. I couldn't let go of that."

"But you were about to make your dream come true."

"Well, my dream is this now." Her voice is marred by resignation.

"Is it?" I ask.

"The *army* wasn't everything you ever dreamed of, I'm sure," she says with a scowl. "Life isn't some childhood fantasy. You take whatever happens to you. We just gotta deal with it."

I exhale harshly because I don't have a dream anymore. However, I'm not as jaded as her. Serving overseas roughed me up a bit, sure.

But I believe in making a good future, not calling it a day and waiting for life to slowly roll past me. I'm still chasing the sun and wishing for those fireflies because every day could be my last.

"You never told me your sister got married," I say, changing the subject.

She gives me a curious glance. "I thought you were over her?"

I think about my encounter with Kelsey. I'm still fucking furious at me for dating her.

"Nah, it's been over, but it surprised me to see her here, and married."

"She was pretty shitty about the breakup...and everything," Kaitlynn says. "That's Kelsey. She doesn't like confrontation or long-term commitments. I'm still impressed that she's married."

Why the fuck does she sound so bitter? Wait— "You're upset with her?"

"Of course, I am. It was Kelsey's responsibility to take *Blythe's*. She couldn't stop telling me it was her right as a fucking first born. She drove it to the ground and then, she dumped the carcasses on me."

I look around trying to understand what she's saying, but everything looks fine.

"So, what happened to the show?"

She shrugs while twisting a lock of her long hair. "I couldn't hack it. But that was a long time ago. This is great. I love it."

Kaitlynn sounds content, even cheerful. If I didn't know her, I'd believe her, but I can see behind her façade. I can tell by the way her nose scrunches and her left brow arches that something is bothering her.

It bothers me that she's unhappy. That I can't do anything to make her feel better.

"Miss Blythe, we need you in the kitchen," one of her waiters tells her as he approaches the table.

"Thank you, Pete," she says, then turns toward me. "I hate to eat and run but—"

"It's getting late for me too." I pull out my wallet. "Thank you for everything. How much do I owe you?"

"Ollie, you offend me. I invited you to my house to eat." Then she winks. "But if you ever feel like dining outside you can come over—and *pay*."

"The first one is free," I joke.

She smirks indulgently. "Just promise you'll come back to visit while you're in town."

We rise from our seats, I lean forward and kiss her on the cheek. "I promise. I'll be back soon, and maybe we can go out sometime."

"Of course," she agrees before walking away.

As I leave the restaurant, I glance toward the kitchen door one last time. It sucks that Kaitlynn didn't reach her dreams. I wish she had. She always wanted to be the next Julia Child. Fucking Kelsey.

She's a selfish woman who doesn't give a single fuck about who she hurts. But I'm glad Kaitlynn is here. I'll swing by later, and maybe we can rekindle our friendship. Or should I keep my distance until this attraction I'm feeling is gone? It must be all the years I've been away from her or the lack of sex. Maybe keeping my distance is what's best for both of us.

When I turn on the engine of my car, the image of her beautiful face comes back into my mind. There's something about her that I can't put my finger on and can't get enough of.

I want to reach for her.

Touch her.

But I don't think I will.

She's like the stars: beautiful but unattainable.

And I'll probably never get close enough to either. Yet ... I'm tempted to try.

TEN

Kaitlynn

"WHY DID I let you drag me to class?" I groan as I set up my yoga mat on the floor.

"Because you seemed stressed last night." Paige, my best friend, says as she rolls her eyes.

"Stress is my middle name," I remind her.

"I thought it was Hope, but whatever floats your boat."

Paige has been my best friend since we were in diapers. We understand each other as if we were soul sisters. When she needs me, I'm there for her, and when I need her, she's always there to lend an ear.

Besides being single cat ladies, we both own restaurants. She's more fun at home binge-watching Grey's Anatomy with a bottle of wine, but I hate it when she drags me to yoga. I can't believe she bribed me with her famous chess pie.

"I'd rather be famous than flipping flapjacks all day," I say.

"What do you need to make that happen, honey?"

"Buy my restaurant, that should take all the stress out of my life," I joke.

"Really? After all the years and hard work?" she asks.

I sigh. "Seems like all my hard work hasn't paid off. The staff is always changing, I have a crowd on the weekends, but during the week the place is empty. I'm sure if I build a patio in the back and renovate the place something would change, but …"

"What did Carl say about the renovations?"

"I haven't called him yet. Maybe selling it would be for the best," I admit. Dumping more money into that pit seems pointless.

What would my parents think about me giving up their life's work? It feels like I'm letting the entire Blythe family down, all the way back to my great-grandfather who built the place.

"But it's part of what makes Knox Ridge home," she says.

"Because you love it" I say. "It's not like we're doing anything unique or cool, especially with your bakery being as good as it is."

Paige's SweetCakes is the best bakery in Knox Ridge. It's one of the best bakeries in the whole entire state, for that matter.

Mom helped her get started and she's been my rock ever since my parents died.

"Good morning, ladies, and welcome to Yin Yoga class," the instructor calls from the front of the class. "I'm Aberdeen, and I'll be your guide for the next sixty minutes."

"Ugh, I hate the transplants," I sigh. "Why do they keep moving here?"

"Change is good, asshole," Paige says. "Stagnation is death and Knox Ridge could use some new bodies."

"Maybe…" I say and frown.

She's right, I am being a bitter asshole. It's just hard to be welcoming to new people when they take so much of what we do here for granted. They only know a quarter of our story at best. It makes it hard to stomach when they filter through Blythe's as if it were a tourist attraction instead of a restaurant.

AFTER CLASS, my muscles are screaming in agony. I should use them a little more often ... either that or stop letting Paige drag me to these things. After taking a shower, I go from barely feeling my limbs to aching all over as I start to change into my regular clothes. I have to run by the restaurant before the laundry service gets there. Then, I need to start prepping for the Monday night sit down.

Every Monday, I close the restaurant to the general public, so I have the morning off and can then feed the less fortunate in our community. There are plenty of families in the area who've owned their houses for generations but live on food stamps and work three plus jobs to make ends meet. It's not much, but everyone deserves a hot meal made for them.

"I'll help you with the renovations," Paige offers.

"Then, you'll buy it?" I say hopefully.

If Paige took the restaurant off my hands, I could get back to my real life. My old boss might still take me back.

"You of all people should know that I couldn't keep up with Blythe's *and* my bakery," she says, crushing my dreams. "What would you do after you sold it anyway?"

I have so many ideas. I just don't know what I'd do first.

"Be like Marcy and Clark?" I say. "Their YouTube channel has millions of followers. Their sponsorship supports them and their annual trips. Maybe I won't be Rachel Ray or Paula Deen, but I could be *like* them."

I recall the time I was with Ollie in Tybee island talking about the world. For a moment, I toyed with the idea of traveling with him for months at a time, discovering everything around. But always coming back home. He didn't want that. Not the trips, nor the home —nor me.

Ollie wanted his freedom from the town. He fought for it, literally. Yet, he's back here. For how long?

"Traveling will be nice," I say, trying to forget Oliver Tanner and the wishes I wasted on him while I was growing up with him.

"Well then, start your YouTube channel, and you can do both," she argues.

"I could if my kitchen wasn't outdated and barely working."

The stove is as old as I am, and I'm pretty sure if the refrigerator were a cat it'd be on its ninth life by now.

"We go back to 'fix that restaurant.' Get her perky and kicking again. People will flock for miles the second they hear about a grand-reopening at Blythe's," Paige says.

Fuck, if only it were that easy.

"C'mon, it's begging for some fucking juice. Can't you hear it? It's crying 'save me, Katy. I feel so cold.'"

I roll my eyes at her antics. "Let's say that I do, and then what? I just start doing cooking segments and posting them online? Hope burning at both ends helps me break even?"

"Or get enough revenue to hire a team to do the day to day stuff," she says. "Blythe's would be a lot nicer with you in one place at a time instead of trying to be in ten."

That's ... not a bad idea, honestly. I mean, how many people are famous from filming content in the comfort of their own homes?

"Maybe I could," I think out loud. "While Kelsey's still in Georgia, I can delegate some of my responsibilities to her."

"She's in town?" Paige asks in obvious disbelief.

Kelsey isn't Paige's favorite person ... Kelsey isn't *most* people's favorite person. But she's my sister. So it's not like I can get rid of her, even if I wanted to.

I want to so bad.

"For a couple of weeks, maybe a month," I say. "She came to help me with the restaurant—not that she's done much. John is here, and so far, they've had a billion excuses to travel up and down Georgia while forgetting all about me."

She promised to help until I hire more part-time staff for the weekends. But so far, all she's given me is a few lame excuses and a headache.

I decide to bring up Ollie, preferring to deal with that than the topic of my sister.

"Did you hear that Oliver Tanner is back in town?"

She squints. "Why does that name sound familiar?"

"Josey Tanner's son," I say, unamused by her attitude.

Paige wrinkles her nose. "Little Ollie AWOL? Showing his face back here? That idiot?"

I hate when she refers to him as that. I hold back a frustrated groan. I don't need more reminders of how he left me here—embarrassed and heartbroken.

It's not like they were friends or anything, I think sarcastically. Then again, she's always the first person to remind me that he broke my heart—twice.

"Yeah, that one," I say dryly, regretting the subject. "He's staying at the old Tanner place while he decides what to do with his life."

"He's going to fuck up my hydrangeas, isn't he?" Paige says.

"So not the point," I say.

"Is he as hot as I remember him?" she asks.

I smirk. Oliver is good looking. He has tousled brown hair, which is thick and lustrous. His eyes are a mesmerizingly deep brown, and flecks of amber light dance throughout them. Like fireflies. His face is strong and well defined. His features look like they were molded from granite. He has thick eyebrows, which slopes downward in a severe expression.

My stomach does a few flips as I remember his playful smile. My body shivers, remembering the tingles that his strong hands created when they touched me. They were rough but warm. And when those beefy arms wrapped around my body, it felt perfect.

His body was toned and inviting as he hugged me. Everything about him was comforting. His voice was deep and rich. We saw each other a couple of days ago, but I'm still thinking about him.

His laugh is gruff but light, like the roar of a freshly tuned engine. It was a relief to hear it. It reminded me of the way we've always been so comfortable with each other. I wished he hadn't left, or that he had come back sooner. The sound of the locker doors opening and closing snap me out of my musings.

"He's alright," I say, casually tucking a bit of hair behind my ear.

Paige crosses her arms. "Uh huh, and Chris Evans is an ugly farmhand."

I blush furiously. "You noticed that too, huh?"

She chuckles, still staring at me like she's expecting a five-page essay on his stubble—*it was so sexy.*

"Well this has been exhausting and humiliating," I say lightly. "Gotta run. Maybe next we could skip the cardio and work on our glutes?"

Paige rolls her eyes. "For the last time, sitting on a couch isn't exercising anything."

"One of these days I'll prove you wrong." I wink before pushing the locker room door open.

Oliver

AT FOUR IN THE MORNING, I jump out of bed, throw on a pair of sweats, a t-shirt, and go out for a run. My mind is thrumming with energy. From everything I've heard from other retired soldiers, the best thing to do is tire myself out before the anxiety sets on my chest and I have a nervous breakdown.

Maybe taking Frimston's offer isn't as crazy as I thought. I could at least find out more about the company, the salary they are offering and see what other benefits they have. Maybe Striker is right and they can help me find my way back to civilian life.

As I hit the streets, I scan the premises. The world is almost silent. My senses are on high alert, taking in new information from my surroundings with every step.

I take Main Street. Outside, the same sidewalk that will bustle in a few short hours is quiet, the concrete oblivious to whether it is midday or midnight. The birds are already singing. Some cars are cruising along with their headlights cutting through the early fog.

The mist keeps my skin wet and cold as I pound through the streets. It's chilly for July, but once the sun comes up, the thought of a cool morning will become a distant memory. I spot a truck outside *Blythe's*.

My survivor instinct kicks in right away. As I approach, I see Kaitlynn is beside it, holding some papers and bobbing her head.

"What are you doing here so early, Kit Kat?" I ask when I reach her.

She jolts, then looks at me. "Oliver, didn't expect to see you around."

"That's all for today, Miss Blythe." The guy in the truck jumps out and stands next to Kaitlynn. "Do you need anything else?"

"The produce looks perfect, all fresh. I think it's all good." She glances around the crates and then back at him. "Thank you."

"You need any help hauling it inside? I can offer you a hand," the guy says with a flirty tone.

"I'll help her," I say glaring at him.

She yawns. "You don't have to. I can take care of this myself. I do it all the time."

I take a closer look at her. She looks worn out. The way she slouches against the crates of fruit while fighting to keep her eyes open. The bags under her eyes look like they have bags of their own. They're swollen and almost purple. It makes me wonder how much makeup she piles onto her face every morning.

"What time did you get home last night?" I ask.

"Two-ish?" She picks up one of the boxes making her way to the restaurant.

I pick up the rest and follow behind her.

"You look like you need to go back to bed."

"If I could, I would," she says slowly, rubbing her eyes. "But that's not possible."

"How often do you do this?"

"Every day, I close between one and two and have to be back at four to receive the produce, or the catch of the day or ..." She shrugs.

I shake my head. This isn't right. A restaurant takes a large staff to make it work. There's managers, accountants, and administrators that can be paid to do things like this. She's the owner, she should be delegating work out to trusted employees, not shouldering all the responsibility on her own.

How is she managing this place?

Kaitlynn helped her parents, but she trained to be a chef—and a television producer. She doesn't have a business degree and never cared to learn that part of the restaurant business.

Perhaps, I should find out how she's managing this place. There has to be some way I can help her run it more smoothly. She can't continue dragging herself out of bed within a couple of hours of going to sleep.

Will she let me?

ELEVEN

Kaitlynn

I'm elbow deep in pasta dough when my phone rings. It's the start of the Friday night rush. My staff is shorthanded, *again*, and few people have the number to my personal cell.

I put down the dough, already glaring in my phone's direction. Reading the caller ID makes my blood boil.

It's Kelsey.

"Where are you?" I hiss instead of saying hello. "You were supposed to be here at noon to help with lunch."

"John wanted to go to the aquarium. Traffic is so bad here. We're planning on staying the night and heading over in the morning."

"Atlanta is three hours away," I argue. "I could still use you at eight. This crowd isn't getting any smaller."

"It's five in traffic," she says casually, as if we're talking about the weather. "Anyway, I'm sure you're doing fine without me. You're way better at that chef thing."

I barely hold back a groan. So, it's going to be one of those days with Kelsey.

"But I need you here to wait tables, not cook."

"Gross," she says. "I'm not a stupid teenager anymore, Kaitlynn. You really can't expect me to put on a uniform and let creepy old men ogle me."

"When has that ever happened?"

"It could happen," she insists. "I'm a hot commodity in New York. People love me up there."

"If they love you so much, why are you even down here?" I ask sarcastically.

"Because my baby sister needs my help," she says innocently.

I huff, pinching the bridge of my nose. *Does she think I'm an idiot?*

"What's the real reason, Kelsey? Don't waste my time by pretending you care about this restaurant...or me."

I hear her sighing. "Ugh, fine. My rent went up and we need more cash to cover the difference."

"I thought your place was rent controlled," I say.

"Yeah, apparently the landlord thought I was single. Which is why it *was* so cheap to live there," she explains.

I want to bang my head on the metal counter, but that would fuck up my noodles.

"I really don't have time for this, Kelsey," I say tersely. "You want money? Get your butt down here and earn it."

"But Katy—"

"No buts," I say. "I'm not mom, and you're not a fucking child. Get it together and help me or go home."

I imagine her face turning a deep shade of red as she screams, "You think you're so great carrying on Mom and Dad's little pet project? You're just too pathetic and scared to do something real with your life, Kaitlynn. Why don't *you* get a fucking grip?"

She hangs up before I can argue further. For the next few

minutes, I finish slicing the pasta as quickly as I can. Before I do something stupid, like close the restaurant and go home to plan my big move out of here.

I love Knox Ridge, but on days like today, I want to pack my things and run. I could chase my dreams. Everyone I know has done that. Well, except Oliver who seemed a little lost when he came to visit.

Focus on the restaurant, I order myself. Organizing the next few orders, I realize it's been a few days since Ollie came to visit—a week. Two since he was outside the restaurant, helping me with the produce.

But who's counting?

He hasn't come by or contacted me since.

He promised to come by and instead he just ... disappeared. Maybe we outgrew each other after all these years sending letters back and forth—although we stopped after my parents died. I wouldn't be surprised if Josey call me one of these days asking me to empty her garage because he's selling the house.

I bet he wouldn't contact me. Why would he want to be around me or even speak to me?

Maybe we aren't as close as I once thought. Maybe he expected someone more like the image he built in his mind while stuck in the desert. Perhaps he was hoping to find some exciting career woman or the same old Kaitlynn he left here.

But instead, he found...this. A burnt-out restaurant owner with no job security or concrete future. Nothing is interesting or inspiring about who I've become.

I suppose I misunderstood the pleasant visit we had. For a moment, I thought I was getting my old friend back. A fire sparked inside me. He breathed some life into mine. But it was just for a moment, and the moment is over.

Maybe our friendship is going to be different now, or perhaps it's over.

Is that why I keep thinking about him and his delicious body?

I mean, he's gotten hotter while he was away. The little crush I once had grew several sizes after seeing him. *Little crush?*

You were in love with him, I remind myself. *Deeply, madly, crazy in love. Stay away before he hurts you—again.*

But how can I when something in him awakens my sensual side which has been asleep for months...years really.

When was the last time I got laid?

It was probably my ex, Connor. But that was back in Atlanta. We said we'd try long distance, but quickly drifted apart until we were out of touch and each other's lives completely. None of my relationships have worked out so far.

Oliver predicted that would happen because I was dating douchebags. He never had anything good to say about Steve, Harvey, Sam, *or* Connor, despite not meeting a single one of them in person. Oliver didn't have a good thing to say about any relationship since Kelsey dumped him.

Poor Ollie. She did a number on him. I can't believe no one has snatched him off the market. He's not your typical guy. He's calm under pressure, and he's always there when you need him. Well, he used to be until I really needed him.

But I know he's the kind of person who knows something's wrong from a thousand miles away. Who wouldn't want to be with him?

I tell you who, you.

He can make any day brighter just with a simple text message or a letter. Not that I've received either one from him in a long time.

Who the fuck am I kidding?

This is what I've been trying to tell you. Wake up and smell the horseshit. That guy will never love you the way you love him.

It's not just that, he's not my friend anymore. My chest tightens, and my shoulders sag. Our friendship has been over for a long time. Instead of sulking and thinking about what I've lost, I continue working.

Not that what I'm doing is technically accurate. Between Oliver and Kelsey blowing me off—*again*—I can't get these orders right.

I decide to get myself together by poking my head out of the kitchen. Waiting on tables is a good enough distraction. It's like second nature to me.

Pouring a glass of water at one table, taking empty plates from another, and by the time I get to some of the regulars to help the staff out, I feel a little more centered. I get into an easy rhythm, checking in with one of my recent hires to nudge her in the right direction.

Once I feel like everything is under control, and the front is a little less congested, I run back to the kitchen to check on the takeout orders. No one is keeping an eye on them. For a few minutes, I help pack some of them while giving a hand to the cook. I grab the bags that are ready and head toward the bar.

I bustle out of the kitchen, but before I even get to the bartender, I see *him*. Ollie is here. I want to go and say hello. But before I can do that, Bryan, one of my waiters, approaches me.

"Lori just quit," he says casually but those three words feel like stabbing knives.

"What do you mean she just quit?" I draw a long breath. "She can't do that. Can't she wait until Sunday night?"

I hold back a scream.

Is she trying to kill me? Can't she at least take me with her? Doesn't she realize that if she can't handle a section as small as the one I gave her, this place will fall apart?

I sure as fuck can't handle this restaurant all weekend without her.

Fucking Lori, if I had a nickel for every time someone's kid or grandkid bailed on me, I could afford to leave this place with a manager by now. I should know better than to listen to a regular's personal reference.

They're so reliable, they always say. Yeah, and that's why they need a job, because they can't keep one for too long.

"Everything okay?" Oliver's low sweet voice cools me down just enough to control my anger.

"One of our girls just quit," Bryan informs.

Oliver huffs, his nostrils flaring. He scans the front of the restaurant before looking back at me. "What's her section?" he asks.

"She's in charge of four," I tell him. "The northeast corner."

He walks away to the kitchen and comes back wearing an apron and starts filling orders. I stare at him for several seconds, dumbfounded. My heart does a couple of flips inside my chest.

How could he do that?

Pitching in like it's no big deal and moving around like he owns the place. And looking hot as fuck. To be fair, he probably knows this restaurant as well as I do. But that doesn't mean he needs to go charging in to save the day like some—

Out of the corner of my eye, I see his charming smile glinting as he greets his first table. His perfect lips framing his perfect teeth. They look plush and firm, and right for kissing. His t-shirt covers his muscular arms like a second skin, letting his exquisitely tattooed lines peek through. He looks like a regular—

... Knight in shining armor. I shake my head, snapping myself out of this strange daze.

There's something about Oliver that's intoxicating, mesmerizing even. His presence is commanding yet comforting. He's always had a way with taking charge that can be endearing at the best of times and exasperating at the worst.

He's so sweet and thoughtful and emotionally mature.

Ugh! I can't believe he's for real.

I shiver, giving him one last glance. He seems to have everything covered. He's even greeting some of the tables near his section, clearly picking up the slack for everyone else. I quietly walk back to the kitchen ambivalent, but glad to know I can go back to cooking in relative peace.

TWELVE

Oliver

When I worked at *Blythe's*, Fridays and Saturdays were the best. The place was always busy, and the tourists were big tippers. I see that the crowd hasn't diminished, but the service isn't as great.

Kaitlynn has only two waiters working for her. The kitchen is understaffed too. She's trying to do everything at the same time. Even though she keeps a smile on her face, I can see the frustration in her eyes.

When my section is under control, I make the rounds, trying to keep the place running and helping her where I can.

"Thank you," she whispers as we walk together to the kitchen. "Not sure what I'd have done tonight."

"What happened?"

"As you saw, one person quit earlier, and Kelsey decided to go visit the aquarium and can't make it back to work. I bet she's going to ask me for her pay when the month is over."

"Pay?"

"She came to help me and earn a little extra," she explains.

"Kelsey doesn't work?"

"They both teach at a high school in NYC. He's old money. A trust fund baby, at least that's what she said. They're always falling short. Supposedly, they have savings to survive the summer, but when she needs extra she comes down here to work for me. Except, she doesn't work as much as I need her to...or at all, really."

"Order for ten is ready," the cook says.

"That's me," she says. "Holler if you need me."

Fucking Kelsey. She hasn't changed.

When the next order comes up, I put it on my tray and head back out. For the next few hours, we work together to get the restaurant under control. Afterward, I help Kaitlynn with closing.

"You hungry? I can whip us up something," she says once the floors are swept and the chairs are put away.

"I've been eating the food that I ordered during the few breaks I was able to take," I reply while adjusting the tables.

"Well, I think we're done for tonight." She exhales loudly, crossing her arms. "Thank you for helping me."

"I'll walk you to your car," I offer.

"You don't have to. This area's pretty quiet."

"Still, let me follow you home so I can make sure you're okay. Here, program your number into my phone."

As I walk her to her car I ask, "Do you need help tomorrow?"

"I don't want to impose."

"Hey, it's me," I remind her. "You're not imposing."

She looks at me cautiously. "If you don't have a hot date or anything, I'd say yes, please."

"I'll be here tomorrow at lunch." I kiss her cheek before closing her door for her.

I get in my car to follow her home. Eventually, she parks in front of the old Montgomery complex. She gets out of her car, waving at me before disappearing into one of the buildings. I continue to stare, long after she's out of sight.

Kit Kat: *Thanks again for today. You saved my sanity.*
Ollie: *Have a good night.*

THE NEXT MORNING, I wake up at the same time—four. I go out for a long run and when I'm done take a detour to Paige's Sweet-Cakes. What a ridiculous name!

Only Paige could come up with something so…Paigy.

I have no idea what to expect. Like Katy, the last time we saw each other she was a kid. Mom kept me up to date on what the girls were up to—that's what she called Kaitlynn and Paige. The only thing I know about Paige is that her bakery is the best.

"If you ever go to Knox Ridge, she has the best coffee and her pastries are just like Nana's," she told me.

"Look what the cat dragged," a woman behind the counter says.

She's petite, dark hair and those sparkling amber eyes are gazing at me with amusement.

"What happened to you?" I toss my head back laughing. "You look like a real person."

"I grew up, dork," she says. "You haven't changed much. Still looking stupid. At least you didn't die."

"It's good to see you haven't changed that much. How are your parents?"

"Still traveling." She shrugs. "Mom won't stop until Dad retires. Or…maybe she just doesn't want to retire. Who knows? Since neither one has to come home to check on their daughter, I barely see them these days."

That's the one thing we shared. Absent parents, well, and the Blythes. They were our family. Richard and Cynthia didn't watch us as a favor to their friends, but because they loved us as their children.

"You're here to stay?"

"I'm not sure yet," I confess.

"You do something stupid and this time I'll kill you, Oliver Tanner. I don't fucking care if you're taller and meaner. You fuck up again and this time I won't have mercy on you."

I glare at her and shake my head.

"You're still weird."

She laughs. "Well obviously."

The bell above the door rings, we both turn to look at who arrives and is Striker.

"Morning, Miss Williams," he greets Paige, nodding at her once. Then turns to look at me. "Tanner."

"Peach muffin and a double espresso, Lieutenant Frimston?" Paige asks with a weird tone that I'm pretty sure is flirty.

"Yes, ma'am."

The gazes they exchange makes me shiver. Seriously, is he fucking flirting with Paige? She's like my little sister. Isn't there a code that says he can't be doing this? At least not in front of me. It's disgusting.

If they're going to flirt, they should at least cut out the crap of Ms. Williams and Lieutenant Frimston.

I stare at both of them and shake my head. "Striker, have you met Paige?"

"We did," he clears his throat. "I do."

Striker who is outgoing and never has trouble speaking stutters and looks away from Paige.

"Paige, would you like to go out on a date with Striker?"

"Striker, you could pick her up tomorrow around..." I check on her store hours which are posted on the board. "Four, maybe take her to Tybee island or Atlanta?"

He rubs his neck. Paige's red as a tomato. She turns around to get a muffin and the espresso she offered Striker. I grab them and say, "get the same for him. It's your turn to pay, Frimston."

"I mean it, Oliver Tanner. You do something stupid and your mother won't recognize you when I'm done with you."

"It's good to see you Paige."

Whatever she's talking about isn't any of my concern. I leave the bakery but sit by one of the tables she has outside the shop. I take a bit of the muffin and realize Mom is right. It's like eating Nana's muffins. Warm, soft and they melt in your mouth. It reminds me of Kaitlynn's cooking too. All the memories of our childhood hit me all at once. From the moment we drove into town to the time I drove away.

What would Nana say if I ask her about my future?

She was wise and loving.

I chuckle. She'd drag me by the ear into the house and say, "where have you been all this time, Oliver Tanner. About time you're back home. Now fix this town, because that's what Blythes do."

"What was that?" Frimston says when he takes a seat.

"What was what?"

"You set me up on a date with Paige Sweet Cakes."

I shake my head. "Is that supposed to mean something?"

"She's going to eat me alive."

"You're older than her."

"So?"

"What's the problem?"

"First, tomorrow I have to meet with my employer."

He takes a sip of his coffee and frowns. "You should come with me," he says. "The second part is…I'm not ready to go out with her. We're just getting to know each other."

"You're kidding right? You fought a war, but you're scared of that woman?"

He shrugs. "I just want to get it right, you know."

"As you wish but be careful though. You hurt her and I'll kill you. She's like my kid sister."

"Like Katy Blythe?" He asks.

I shake my head and wave my hand. We're not discussing Kaitlynn. "So, what's tomorrow?"

"We're going to Oregon. It's a training session. You can at least meet the guys. As I said, we could use a guy like you."

After tossing the last piece of muffin in my mouth, I nod.

"Let me think about it." I rise from my seat and leave.

EVER SINCE I CAN REMEMBER, the Blythes always cooked for the staff before they opened, and that hasn't changed. Kaitlynn made us Black Pepper Shrimp with collard greens and blackberry cobbler. Her other two waiters eat quietly at a table next to us while we shoot the breeze.

"I feel like you want me to hire you, Tanner," she jokes. "Two days in a row. Are you keeping track of your hours?"

"No," I say with a shrug. "The tips are enough."

"Are you sure?"

"Believe me, I'm doing this for selfish reasons. Damn woman, your cooking is delicious."

"If you want, I can pack up some of the leftovers for you to take home," she offers.

"I'll take anything you want home," I insinuate with a smirk, reaching for her hand.

Her cheeks flush. When I realize what I said, I quickly snatch my hand away, grabbing our empty plates before rushing awkwardly to the kitchen. As I'm scraping the excess food into the garbage disposal, I hear her voice behind me.

"Are you alright?" she asks. "You're acting a little weird."

"Totally fine," I lie. "Just tidying up before opening."

I look over my shoulder, noticing her glare at me. After a moment, she sighs.

"Okay, then." She slouches and walks away.

This attraction feels like a wall between us. I can't act on it. Yet I can't seem to shake it off.

Don't do anything stupid, Tanner!

You have no idea what to do with your life. She's in a bad place. What would you accomplish by acting out of lust?

Things pick up quickly once the lunch rush starts, and the awkwardness of earlier fades. I'm in charge of two sections today since Kelsey's "stranded" in Atlanta. Fuck knows how that's possible.

The other cook doesn't arrive until five, so Kaitlynn's responsible for the kitchen until then. Things seem to be going relatively smoothly. The crowd starts to wane around 2pm, and that's when I hear a strangled scream coming from the back. I rush to the kitchen to see what's wrong.

I find Kaitlynn with her head inside one of the ovens. She's talking to it as if it were a person.

"C'mon, Gerty," she says frankly. "I know I promised to replace you. I know I promised you a nice little retirement. If you could just...fucking...pull it together for one more weekend, I promise you'll never have to work in this stinking town ever again."

"That's a lot to ask of an old lady," I joke.

She backs out of the oven, turning to glare at me like I'm hellspawn.

"Stay out of this, Tanner," she hisses. "This is between me and this bitch."

"I'm sure the sweet talking is helping a lot." I swallow the laugh. She's fucking adorable when she's upset. "But what Gerty might need is a tune up."

"Thanks for the wisdom, Thomas Edison," she barks. "Don't you think I've tried that?"

"Maybe you need a second pair of eyes," I suggest as I bend down next to her. "I happen to have a working set right here."

She glares, but a moment later her shoulders sag and she nods, scooting over to allow me to inspect the oven. I do a once over, pretending to inspect it, before heading to the office. I grab the toolbox out from underneath her father's old desk.

It takes me a few minutes of tweaking, but eventually I get everything tight enough in the back. Then I try turning it on, leaving the oven door open to see if it's working at all. After a few seconds, heat starts spilling from the open compartment.

I chuckle quietly. "See?" I tell Kaitlynn. "Gerty isn't a nasty old woman. She just needed a little love."

"She's just being nice with you because she's a horny old hag," she argues. "Maybe if I feed you to her, she'll run smoothly for a whole year."

"Ha, ha," I let out a humorless laugh. "I'm sure it'll be fine when you swap her out with a new one."

"Well here's hoping it's that easy," she says.

"Why wouldn't it?" I frown. "She's broken. Just get a new one."

"Are you really that naïve?" Kaitlynn slaps the oven, making a resounding boom echo through the kitchen.

I stare at her. "What?"

"Let me pretend for two seconds that I can afford to get a brand-new oven from this century any time soon," she says. "Let's pretend that throwing some money at the flashiest new gadget would be feasible. That's completely ignoring the fact that this kitchen is older than I am. Do you think I'll be able to cram a new oven in here that can run with wiring that hasn't been updated since maybe the 70s?"

I hadn't considered that. "What do you want me to say? That it's hopeless? That we shouldn't even try?"

She sighs, shaking her head. "I just wish people would stop giving me that 'one simple solution' they have to fix the one thing that's not working that day. It's not just the oven, or the toilets, or the..."

She stands up as she continues, "...It's the electric, and the fridge, the paint, the floors, the uniforms, the worker retention rate...the infrastructure. It all needs money and fixing and...I'm one fucking person, Ollie."

She's right.

But she shouldn't be doing this all alone. *We* could fix it. I decide to drop it for now because I know we won't get anywhere with this while the restaurant is still open. Her mind is always torn where this place is concerned. I'm not sure if she even knows if she loves it or hates it here.

"You're welcome for the repair, by the way," I say instead.

"Well yeah, thanks," she says with a softer voice and a tired smile. "If she doesn't quit by the end of the night, I'll put her to work baking a reward for you."

"I could think of another reward if she gets too tired," I say with a smirk.

Kaitlynn looks down, blushing. She then glares at me lightly. "Are we still talking about food, Tanner?"

I lick my lips. "Of course we are," I say, composing myself. "But we can discuss that later. I should go check on my tables."

Feeling cowardly, I run away. I sense sweat beading down my neck as I muster a charming smile for one of my tables. Is it the heat of the kitchen, the heat of Knox Ridge, or the radiance beaming off every inch of Kaitlynn's body that has me so hot?

During the next couple of hours, I do some housekeeping to keep my mind occupied. By the time the dinner crowd starts to trickle in, my mind is back to Kit Kat.

Since the second chef has clocked in, the kitchen isn't Kaitlynn's only point of focus. My eyes wander every few seconds, seeking her out like a target hiding in the brush. But instead of an enemy threatening to attack, it's me searching for...a shapely pair of legs and a smile brighter than the sun?

Am I desperate and horny, or does she have me under some kind of spell?

Either way, I might want to stay at home tomorrow, or I won't be able to keep my hands to myself.

The sun set a while ago, but the line for the hostess table is still well past the front door. By now, I have an idea of what this place could use to run smoother. Not to fix the place, but we can start with something small.

We need at least a couple of more servers per shift. More kitchen staff. We could really use a busboy or two. Maybe drinks from the bar wouldn't take so fucking long if the bartender didn't have to handle takeout orders too.

If this was my place, I'd invest in new appliances, staff, and furniture. I'd also do some renovations like repainting the walls and building a patio outside.

This place is a disaster. I can't believe Kaitlynn's kept it open for as long as she has. I have so many questions about this restaurant and how she's managed it so far. But I'll wait until the crowd dies down more.

Sometime later, Kaitlynn approaches me. "Have you taken your break yet?"

"No, it's been crazy," I admit.

"I can cover your tables for a little," she says, nudging me toward the kitchen. "C'mon, you can take a plate and eat in the office."

"Have you eaten yet?" I ask.

She shrugs. "I've had a bite here and there."

"You should be the one taking a break," I say.

She snorts. "It's barely nine, and I've had food. This is an easy night."

Without another word, she heads toward the dining room.

"IS this every night or just this weekend?" I ask after closing.

"Pretty much every night," she says with a strained voice.

I sigh, running a hand through my hair.

"You saved my life again." She grins. "So, thanks for that."

Don't thank me, just tell me how to help you. I can see her sinking along with the restaurant, and no one is around to help her.

"So about renovating this place..." I ask hesitantly.

She glares. "What about it?"

"What's stopping you?"

"Uh, money," she says defensively.

What happened to her inheritance? The Blythes weren't rich, but their restaurant was profitable...it used to be profitable, at least.

"That's what banks are for," I argue. "Have you ever considered applying for a loan?"

"Gee, I never would've thought of that," she says sarcastically. "That's really clever of you, Tanner. I'll just call up the bank right now and see if they've forgiven the last loan I had to take out just to buy Kelsey's half of the restaurant."

"I'm sorry, I didn't know." I rub the back of my head.

"Of course you don't," she says.

"What's that supposed to mean?"

"You've been gone for years, Oliver. What did you expect, to just ride back into town and save me from my shitty little life?"

"Fuck you, I'm not the one who cut me out of their life. That was all you, Kit Kat," I say, glaring at her.

"I didn't cut you out!" Her voice resonates throughout the walls.

"You stopped writing," I accuse her. "You made it pretty clear where I belong in your life."

I don't belong close to the Steves, Sams, Connors, or any of the fucking assholes she preferred to hang out with.

"*I* stopped writing because my parents died. What's your excuse?" She screams, clutching her hair.

I close my eyes briefly. Shit, I hadn't thought of that. I lower my head, avoiding her gaze for a few seconds. I'm a fucking asshole. Why didn't I reach out to her?

As if reading my mind, she crosses her arms. Her smile is triumphant but hollow.

"That's what I thought, you're like everyone else. Waiting at the receiving end," she scolds. "If you were looking for some brownie points for bothering to check up on an old friend, don't worry. I'll let the locals know you're a regular standup guy. No need to keep up pleasantries to fit in around here."

I groan, frustrated. Typical Kaitlynn. She thinks that if someone lets her down once, they're bound to do it again.

One time?

Her parents died years ago and you never checked up on her. You could've visited at least a couple of times and it never occurred to you that she needed you.

"Don't pretend like you know me either," I say quietly.

She takes a step closer to me. Her eyes are defiant but her lip trembles.

"What's that supposed to mean?" she asks tightly.

"Maybe I don't know what you're going through, but I still

know you better than anyone, Kit Kat," I say, tracing my finger along her jawline. "I know all your tells."

"Keep telling yourself that," she rasps quietly, staring at my lips.

I growl. "You're just so ... so ... so ..."

"So what?" she snaps. "So childish? So fucking naïve for trying to keep a hell shack like this open?"

"So stubborn," I end my sentence trying to calm the pent-up emotions I've been gathering since I first saw her a week ago.

"Fuck you, Ollie," she growls, her green eyes opening wide.

There's a fire burning deep within her soul. It's the mark of someone feisty...brave...and every bit as bold as she is beautiful. There's also pain. I want nothing more than to take it as far away from her as possible.

Following my instincts, I lean forward, brushing my lips against hers.

We kiss softly for a few seconds, but the warmth that transpires between us becomes a blazing fire. In no time, it turns from an innocent and playful peck into something deeper.

This kiss is hot, searing with red-hot passion. My hands drift to her hips, squeezing her curves tightly. I pull her closer, her body fits perfectly against mine. She splays her hands against my chest, pushing me away and extinguishing the fire between us with her cold gaze.

"What the fuck is your problem, Tanner?" she shouts.

"I'm sorry," I apologize, my voice weak, needy, lustful. "I was just trying—"

"To what? Get me in bed? Pity fuck me?"

"No. That's—"

"Get out of here," she says, pointing toward the door.

"What?"

I can't leave just like that. She's upset and confused. Just like I am.

"Out! Now!" She screams.

As I am about to say something else, she walks to the entrance and opens the door.

"I can't deal with you, Tanner. Get out of my restaurant."

Without another word, I leave. As I drive home, I can't stop thinking about everything that just transpired between Kaitlyn and me.

Is our friendship over?

I care about my friend, but fuck, I'd be a liar if I say that's all that worries me. After that kiss, I want more.

My lips are still burning with the memory of her sweet ones. My heart is pounding out of my chest. My body feels electrified, and the warmth we created continues to thrum through me. I want a repeat. I want to kiss her again until we fuse as one.

I shouldn't try. She's my best friend. I grew up with her. But a kiss like that is the beginning of a promise. A promise that won't stop until she finds her dream.

THIRTEEN

Kaitlynn

JUST AFTER DAWN is the best time of day. The sun peeks over the top of the hill in the cemetery, kissing everything it touches with a warm ethereal glow.

A thick summer fog hugs tightly to the ground. I take off my shoes as I enter, feeling the morning dew seep into my toes. As the breeze caresses my skin, I exhale deeply, feeling the way life tingles all around.

My eyes wander as I trudge toward the Blythe section of the graveyard. Every gravestone tells a different story. Some with generic sayings like "Loving Mother" and others are more personal about the deceased's life like "Died how they lived, Fighting for others."

The style, size, and stone of the grave markers all have stories to tell about their families, their wealth, and who remembered them after they died.

The Blythes have an illustrious history in Knox Ridge as caretakers and healers. Generations of Blythes have kept this town healthy and well fed. I swallow thickly, gripping the picnic basket in my hand tightly when I arrive at my destination.

"Hey guys," I greet them quietly.

Richard & Cynthia Blythe, it reads. *Lovers, Fighters, Restaurateurs Extraordinaires.*

I chuckle sadly. I added the last part just for dad. He would hate if anyone in town ever forgot how successful *Blythe's* is...was.

I sink to my knees, letting my sandals and picnic basket fall to the ground next to me.

"I brought brunch. Your favorite meal, Mom," I say cheerfully, tucking my legs underneath my skirt before opening the basket.

Mom always liked it when I wore my Sunday best for her. I try to please her, even though it's a Monday and she's six feet under.

"I made turkey bacon, so no one has to worry about their cholesterol levels or blood pressure rising," I joke.

"You'd appreciate the sentiment, Mom," I say. "Dad, I'm sure you're rolling under there."

I quietly set up the blanket, laying out the dishes. I pull out the thermos last. "But don't worry, that's what the Brandy is for."

"Paige gave me some town gossip, but honestly I've been so out of it this week," I admit.

Like always, I chat for a while at the gravestone, talking about the town, the restaurant's regulars, and how Gerty is amazingly still kicking. A knot forms in my stomach the longer I keep talking. I need to put on a happy face. They're dead, but they're my parents, and this is what they'd be most excited about for that week. They deserve a little comfort.

My lips tremble when I finish talking about my neighbor's Rottweiler and how he keeps trying to make friends with my cat. Myrtle is not amused.

I bite into an apple. "I, uh, I'm sorry I didn't have time to come visit last week. It's hard to get out here when I'm still looking for new staff."

Even though they aren't here, I can remember the sad look in my parents' eyes every time I let them down. The way Dad would keep a stiff upper lip, and how Mom would smile with wet eyes. They wanted to be supportive, but in those moments, I felt as if I wasn't enough for them.

It only happened a handful of times while they were alive, but I can only imagine how devastated they'd be if they could see *Blythe's* today.

I lick my lips, staring at my bare feet. "Remember when I was moving to Atlanta? I told you I could maybe help on weekends. But the restaurant wasn't my dream, and it'd never be...I'd never seen you so mad. It was like I ripped your hearts right out of your chests.

"You thought I would come home eventually...but I wanted to figure out what was it about the outside world that made everyone leave, guys. And so far, I've liked it. It was freedom. I could make mistakes, and no one would judge me. Certainly, not the entire town. I know you love this place, but I'm a disaster. I'm losing more money than I'm making as I try to keep this place open.

"I know...you mentioned you wanted me to take over someday and maybe film my show from the restaurant so everyone in the south would know where to go for good comfort food but...but...."

I close my eyes, taking a deep, shuddering breath. "But I can't make *Blythe's* big. I can't even keep it afloat. I know you must hate me for saying this but...some days I really regret taking it from Kelsey. No, maybe I regret letting her sell the house and take over because she was the first freaking born.

"I should've let her fix the mess but...I couldn't let her sell the restaurant too. She wanted to get rid of it, and how could I let her hand over your life's work to some stranger. She did it with our house." I release a big, painful laugh.

That's exactly what I'd love to do just about now.

"I know it was your dream. And...you poured your lives and souls into that place. But I can't," I insist, convincing them—or myself that giving up is for the best.

"Mom, Dad...I'm sorry, that isn't me. I'll never be as good as you. Dad, you always told me that a smart person knew when to quit."

My gaze diverts. I'm a fucking coward, I can't even look at my parents' gravestone as I disappoint them yet again. "I don't think it will ever be even a shadow of what it used to be when you two were alive."

The cicadas are screeching nearby. I wonder who they lose while in hibernation. Maybe they're crying for how much they've lost being stuck in the ground for fifteen years. Maybe they see the same old dirt and have convinced themselves that nothing's changed at all for fear of grief.

"I'm miserable, okay?" I snap. "I don't have time to bake for myself. I have one friend, and I love Paige, but she can't be there for me like you were."

Several times, I open and close my mouth, trying to get some words out. I'm trying to say something to make them understand. It shouldn't matter right? Getting my dead parents' approval after all this time.

As my chest constricts, the tears begin slipping down my cheeks.

"Why does it feel like I'm losing you all over again?" I cover my face, sobbing just like I did when I first got the news of their death.

Kelsey's tactless voicemail replays in my head. "Just so you know, Mom and Dad were in a car accident. The sheriff says they died at the scene. Since you're closer, you should drive down there. I won't be able to fly home until Monday."

My entire world collapsed. I wanted to call Ollie, but how could I when he was out of reach? Everyone I knew wasn't around Knox Ridge when it all happened. Since they passed, it's been me against the world.

Since my parents didn't have a will, Kelsey jumped at the chance to own the restaurant. That didn't last long. Manual labor isn't her thing. I should've stayed in Atlanta, let her deal with the mess she made. Or maybe I should have taken the reins immediately before she let things collapse. If only Ollie had been around.

"You remember Oliver Tanner? He came back into town last week," I try to change the subject, once I'm all cried out. "He, uh, he helped me out me out this weekend when we were understaffed...again. It was nice, you know? To have someone around who knows the kitchen, and the restaurant...and me."

"For the first time in years, I wasn't alone."

I lick my lips again. One of my hands finds its way to the grass. My fingers clench so tightly into the blades that some of them rip right out of the ground. It's calming...in a sick sort of sadistic way. Like for one moment in the messed up history of my adult life, I don't have to suffer alone.

"I know your death was rough on Kelsey too. But fuck, she made a mess of the restaurant. And once she didn't want to play anymore, she left for New York," I continue. "I lost my sister, my parents...my fucking *life*. I just...I know you didn't mean to die, but did you really have to go like that? At the same time?

"It's so hard to act as if this is the life I wanted for myself. I can't begin to describe how much I hate it here...hate myself for hating Knox Ridge," I can hear the panic in my own voice. "Screw things going back to normal, or the way they were before. I want a life, period. This is...it's like I've been gasping for air since you died. Every time it gets a little easier, someone shows up and crushes my lungs."

They feel like they're being crushed right now. I take a deep breath, and then two, and try to remember what being alive is supposed to feel like. Because, during moments like these, I feel as cold as Mom and Dad's lifeless bodies.

"And then Ollie shows up and he's...different," I mutter. "He's changed so much. He's not the same guy who used to be my best friend, or the guy who held my hand when things were hard or sad. Remember when Nana died? He never left my side for days. You even let him stay the night with me."

I sigh because I wished he'd been there when Mom and Dad left. I know in my heart that everything would've been a little less painful.

Hugging my arms, I continue, "I missed feeling like I could *count* on someone other than myself. I forgot what it's like to just do my job, and not everyone else's. Ollie made that happen for a couple of days.

"He even fixed Gerty," I say with a chuckle. "I can't believe that she's still alive.

"That didn't last much. Of course, I had to fuck it up." I huff. "Because I'm Kaitlynn, right?"

I draw a deep breath. "I'm stubborn, and I don't listen, right?"

My eyes are still wet. The feeling only gets worse as I remember our worst fights. They were always about the restaurant. They were always about my fucking future and upholding the family dynasty.

"I pushed him away, and he didn't show up yesterday. Which should be fine but...it really isn't. I don't know how much longer I can keep up with being this person," I tell them, hoping that some-where, they're listening. "I want someone like Ollie to just take me away from here—or make it all better."

Dawn is the best time of the day because there's no chance of anyone else stumbling upon us. No one who will swoop in and pretend to understand my life. It's just me, my parents, and the cicadas—crying for what we've lost and what we'll never find.

"Does wanting to leave make me a bad person?"

FOURTEEN

Oliver

AT FOUR IN THE MORNING, before I go out for a run my phone buzzes. Striker Frimston reads the screen. When I unlock the screen it reads, *I'm picking you up in ten.*

I grunt.

There're too many things stopping me from taking a job that'll be shipping off to who the fuck knows. My first thought is Kaitlynn. The kiss. It wasn't enough. In that moment, I wanted more than just a kiss. I wanted to suck her into me, inhale her. Become one with her.

So many lost opportunities. If I could go back in time, I would do so many things differently. But life has taught me that there's no such thing like do overs or time machines.

You have to work with what you have and use your mistakes as learning moments. Not bitter regrets.

The doorbell stops my train of thought. That was less than ten minutes. I check to see who is as crazy as Striker to be up this early. It's him.

"You're not ready," he says, pushing the door open.

"Look, I haven't figured out what I want to do but—"

"Just come with me for one day. We can use some of your intel. If this isn't for you, they'll pay you generously for whatever information they need from you."

I shake my head.

"This house could use some renos, that money could come in handy."

I nod, not telling him that money is the last thing I need. Mom married a rich guy. He's smart with money and helped me invest my salary. It's the best he could do for Mom, make sure her son would have financial stability once he retired. He's also expecting me to work for him.

"Tanner, it's just a meeting."

"I'm done being away from home," I answer honestly.

He grins. "Who said you have to be away? We only move when there's a mission. Just hear them out. They pay generously—unless it's for a good cause. Then, you work pro-bono and reject the payment for the greater good."

Without a word, I go to my room to change. It's just a meeting and I'll get Frimston of off my back. If anything, whatever they pay me today would go to Blythe's. That place could use a lot more than some TLC.

HIB isn't just like any company. My first clue is the helicopter waiting for us by the highway. No, the guy waiting for Frimston's car, promising to have it back when he texted. The second clue is the private jet we board in Atlanta. The equipment is better than the one we had in our base. Seven hours after I receive the text, we land on a private runway.

Four men wait for us at the bottom of the staircase.

"Frimston," the tallest one with light bronzed skin nods. "You took longer than we planned."

"Blame your pilot. He arrived later than we agreed." Striker shrugs and gives him a pat on the back. "Good to see you, T."

They look familiar, then again, I have worked with hundreds of men who I can't recognize.

"Guys, meet Oliver Tanner," Frimston introduces me. "Cap, meet HIB. Mason Bradley, Anderson Hawkins—we call him Hawk. Santiago Cordero—we call him T, and Harrison Everhart."

"They call me asshole," Harrison Everhart says with a grin, extending his hand. "Pleasure to finally meet you, Captain."

We exchange a few polite handshakes until Mason Bradley says, "how much did he tell you?"

"I figured I'd let you do all the talking," Frimston said.

Bradley and Hawkins step closer to me. Hawk waves at the other two and say, "we'll see you at the training range."

Who the fuck knows where they brought me. I only know that we're close to the northwestern part of the country. We're far away from any town and other than manmade runaway, there's nothing in a two-mile radius.

Everything around is a sea of evergreens and fog. I'm in the middle of Oregon, or maybe the middle of nowhere. These guys could kill me, bury me and no one would ever know where my body was left.

I wouldn't go down easy though.

"Take it easy, son," Hawk says, squeezing my shoulder. "Relax, we're not the enemy."

I glance at him. He doesn't look old enough to be my father, but whatever he says. I'll relax when I figure out where the fuck I am and how to get out of here alive.

"My father was a Ranger, just like Hawk's dad," Mason starts. "They were brothers in arms. Hawk was a Delta. I trained with Dad, but I liked computers more than I liked the idea of becoming him. Once Dad retired from the force, he began working as a bodyguard for a rock band. Not much, but I learned a lot from that line of work. I found a way to fuse what I learned from him with my computer knowledge. I like the tactical side of being in a mission."

"Videogames," Hawk interrupts him. "That's the way he sees the missions. A strategic video game where he gets to...save the day."

I nod, as if understanding where they are going.

"This started as a small operation," Bradley continues. "I built bolts, installed top of the line alarms and...people call you for all kinds of shit. Now, our company works with other countries, the government, banks, celebrities.

"Everyone needs something, but we don't always accept the job," Bradley says. "I'm particular about my clients. We want to expand and there's a sweet spot close to Knox Ridge where we can set something like this."

"Where are we?"

"On the border of Washington and Oregon," Bradley explains. "No one knows what we do here. It's safe to practice, train and plan. Most of us live in Seattle though. It's close enough to home, but far enough that our families are safe."

"This facility in Knox Ridge?" I ask concerned because he can't think I'll be happy if he puts my family in danger.

"It's far away that your family will be safe." Hawk assures me.

"We need a leader," Bradley says.

"You have Frimston," I remind him.

"He's good," Hawk says and Bradley nods in agreement. "He's not a leader. Captain, we've been keeping an eye on you for years. It's not about the medals, but the way you lead your people during your missions. We need you."

"I can't put Mom or Kaitlynn through this again," I say out loud.

"We have families," Bradley says. "They know what we do can

be dangerous but are also aware that we can die just by crossing the street. You're not going to be moving into the facility. It's just the place where you'll be overseeing the operations when we have a mission. If we don't have a mission, you're free to do as you please. But I'll ask you to have an office for tactical operations."

"How long do these missions last?"

"If you're wondering if you'll have to go underground and infiltrate the mafia?" He laughs. "We have specialized people for that. I want you to help me with intel, planning how we can get a mission done so our men can follow the plan. If I need you on the scene, it'd be like the time you landed in Russia and left within the hour."

"That mission is secret, no one knows about it."

He smirks. "Only the ones who were there."

A light spark inside my head. "You were the private company who consulted with us," I say, finally placing where I had seen these guys before.

Two things happened during that mission. I realized that the war wasn't going to end. There's always something new to fight for and a never ending line of what if's. I had seen the world. More than my fair share of suffering and death. What I've done hadn't changed the world. It had saved lives, but I didn't have the spark inside of me to continue.

Also, I didn't have any more energy to continue fighting. It was time to retire before I made a big mistake.

These guys were able to come in, do the job and leave.

I was stuck waiting for the next orders and hoping it was for the greater good and not some stupid lead taking us to nowhere. This is what I wanted, I remind myself as we continue walking the grounds where they show me the facilities and most of the equipment.

"If I say no, are you planning on killing me?"

"Why would we do that?" Bradley asks.

"You're showing me everything."

"This arrogant bastard never invites someone if he thinks they might say no," Hawk says with a smirk. "It never fails though."

"What makes you think I'll say yes?"

We arrive at an office where there's a map of the world on one side of the wall. Bradley taps on Georgia and says, "do you know this is a hot spot for human trafficking?"

I open my mouth and close it.

"Exactly," he says. "We need a base there and easy access to the Atlantic Ocean. There are bigger wars to fight. Things that our so-called leaders don't even pay attention to because they don't fucking care. There are women and children who get snatched from their families and shipped to other places to become slaves, organ donors, prostitutes. We're seven hours from there...everything would be easier if I have a man I can trust close to this point."

I rub my face and think of all the children I saw while serving in Iraq. Small children missing a leg, an eye or just dead in the middle of the streets because there was no one to save them when a bomb exploded, or they were used as bait.

"Where do I sign?"

"Let's do some training and later today, we can drive up to Seattle. Tomorrow morning we'll discuss your salary and your next steps. I want you to know, this isn't just a team. We're family," Bradley says. "Welcome to our family, Tanner."

FIFTEEN

Kaitlynn

"A LITTLE BIRDIE told me you had some extra help last weekend," Paige says, flashing me her all-knowing grin.

I totally want to kill her. She dragged me here, and now she wants to talk about something I don't even want to think about. Thanks, but no thanks. I feel like I'm going to pass out and it's all her fault.

The air in this stupid yoga studio is so hot, it's as bad as trying to exercise outside in the balmy Georgia sun. Why should I pay extra for something I can get free at the park with my phone? Maybe if I try hard enough, I could die of heat stroke and avoid this awkward conversation.

"No idea what you're talking about," I lie, praying that the ground will swallow me. "You sure it wasn't bad intel from one of the employees you sent to spy on me?"

"Spy is such a strong word," she says as she sets up her mat. "I prefer 'looking out for.'"

I glare humorlessly. "Any chance you could just send one over next time to actually help?"

"I love you, honey, but paying an employee to work for the competition? That's a terrible business strategy."

"Pity, I could use the extra help since Ollie flaked on me yesterday." I snap my mouth closed, realizing the mess I've gotten myself into by letting that little tidbit slip. Now Paige's going to grill me endlessly.

"So it is true," she says excitedly. "You did have some dreamboat picking up the slack."

I frown. "Who said anything about a dreamboat?"

"I may be embellishing a bit. But do you blame me? Oliver Tanner all beefed out and in an apron?" She moans with a playful grin, "Butter me up, and call me a waffle. I'd let him eat me any day."

I wasn't buttered up. More liked greasy and sweaty, and he didn't care...and I almost let him eat me...

"Not funny." I glare at her.

"Good, I'm being serious," she says. "Clearly, you're still hung up on him. So when are you gonna tap that?"

"Are you serious?" I growl. "I can't. It's Ollie."

But since Saturday night, I keep circling back to what almost happened. I can't get him, or the memory of that kiss, out of my head.

The taste remains in my mouth. His presence felt comfortable, but his arms, they felt like home. I don't know what it is about him.

Ollie and I have always shared a connection. We know each other so well. No matter how far away he is, I still feel it. But this time I won't let my heart lead me.

I won't let my guard down.

This time we are old friends who happen to live in the same place—until he leaves again.

"Because...you hate the idea of having a little fun on the side to get him out of your system? Or because you find it hard to believe that a hot, accomplished guy like Oliver Tanner totally has the hots for you?" She asks.

I blush. "Because he's Oliver. He wouldn't take me seriously, even if he wanted something casual."

"...Something happened, didn't it?" Her eyes study me. They're hungry for information.

"Nope," I say weakly. I focus on the door, hoping the instructor will show up any second now to save me from further embarrassment.

"Something totally happened! Look at you, beet red and class hasn't started yet. Ok spill, honey,"

I sigh and stop fighting her. Within minutes, I tell her *everything* about the weekend, the banter, and our sexual tension. But before I can mention the kiss, the yoga instructor, Javier, walks in.

Swallow me, ground.

Javier is... nice to look at, if I'm being honest. He's like a six-foot wall of muscle that's been glazed by the sun brimming with natural charisma and a thick Spanish accent.

"Or, if you want to chicken out of giving me the full scoop, I dare you to fuck that one instead," Paige says.

I wrinkle my nose. "Maybe you're the one who needs to get laid. How are things with Striker? Still playing 1950s courting with him?"

"Shut up."

"You can't be telling me to get some when you're worse than me."

Paige shrugs. "You might be right. But I'm just looking out for your best interests, babe."

"Thanks," I say earnestly. "Just stop trying to set me up with anything that breathes."

"Good morning, class," Javier says with a charming grin. "And hello to you, Katy. Always nice to see you here."

I wave awkwardly.

"See?" Paige whispers. "You wouldn't even have to try to hit that."

"Shut up," I hiss back. It's bad enough that half the class is staring at me like I'm some freak for getting his attention.

Thankfully, Javier begins the class without any more fuss. Or so I hope, because it seems like the class is just for me. I don't appreciate him praising my clumsiness as many times as he does today.

By the time the class is over, I'm ready to sprint out of the room. The sooner I change outfits, the sooner I can get out of here. I'll have to check to see who the instructor is first the next time Paige tries to drag me here.

Hopeful that I escape his attention, I sneak out of the locker room. Only to find him standing right outside waiting expectantly. I'm sure every adult in this town has fantasized about having a night with him. I can't lie and pretend that I've never thought about it.

Javier is interesting and eccentric to say the least. And hot. He has that Rodrigo Santoro vibe going for him.

But after spending enough time around him, I realized that most people in this town can't see past their lust—because Javier is as energetic as he is boring. His beautiful physique is mostly the product of years of boredom. He's a nice guy, but at some point, he has nothing new or stimulating to say.

"Katy, I'm glad I caught you," he says. "I've decided that I'm leaving Knox Ridge."

Well, that's new. Or maybe not, he's filthy rich as far as anyone can tell. From what I've gathered, he only stays in one place for so long, normally a year or two at max. Even when he swore Knox Ridge was where he wanted to settle down, it's always been obvious that we were a little too quiet for him.

"That's sad to hear. Where are you headed?" I try to sound as casual, and unexcited, as possible.

"LA," he says proudly. "A friend of mine is starting a new business venture and I've agreed to partner with him."

"Wow, that's perfect for you," I say. "You'll be missed around here."

Maybe that will keep him occupied and his wandering eyes at bay for a while. I just feel bad for any assistants he might creep out while he's there. He's harmless, but his well-meaning flattery can get out of hand quickly.

"Actually," he says. "That's what I wanted to talk to you about. The venture is revitalizing key properties around the country in order to create authentic American excursions for exclusive clientele."

"That's nice," I say.

It sounds weird, but okay.

"It is. We're very excited," he says enthusiastically. "Which is what I wanted to speak to you about. We've been organizing our pitch to the investors for a few months and, pending the investors' approval, we'd like to make an offer on your restaurant."

"Really?" I say skeptically.

He nods. "It's rustic, one of the oldest houses in the state, oddly enough."

It's like this guy's never picked up a history book.

"So it's old, is that it?" I say, crossing my arms.

"It's close enough to Atlanta for clientele to fly in from all over the world, but it's also deep in the heartland and a short drive from the coast. Besides, can you imagine anywhere more...charming than Knox Ridge?"

I know that by 'charming' h means 'small and in the middle of fucking nowhere.' But I shrug with my hands clasped behind my back to refrain from telling him to go to hell.

"So...what? You buy it off me and turn it into some bed and

breakfast where rich people get to pretend they live in the South for a weekend?"

"Or up to ten days," he says casually. "Whatever they're willing to pay."

I open my mouth to tell him 'thanks, but no.' He immediately starts backing up, saying

"Before you reject my offer," he says, pulling a piece of paper out of his pocket. "Know that we're willing to pay this amount for the building."

I take the paper, reading and rereading it for a moment. There's enough zero's to pay off my debts and move somewhere new. Maybe even enough to buy a house or not work for a year or two.

"Why don't you take a few days to think it over," he says. "Take some time, and then call me when you're ready."

I hesitate for a second, but I swap phone numbers with him. His pitch is mediocre and his business plan sounds creepy. But with that much money and financial security on the line...I'd be stupid not to give him a chance. My phone buzzes a few seconds later.

Before I can pull it out, Javier puts his hand on my arm gently.

"I have another class to teach, but give me a call, Katy. I'd love to do business with you," he says before walking away.

I take a deep breath, my chest squeezing tightly. It isn't too good to be true. It's not even ideal. I wanted to sell the restaurant to a local who could do better by it than I can, not some rich guy who plans on turning Knox Ridge into a tourist trap. But maybe it's the only break I'll ever get. Maybe I should get out now before it's too late.

Maybe this is the sign that I need to move on.

SIXTEEN

Oliver

OLLIE,

I skipped Thanksgiving this year. Mom isn't happy. But I bet she didn't give the same lecture to Kelsey, who also stayed in New York and won't go home for Christmas. I personally don't want to be in Knox Ridge.

There's something missing. The town feels...empty, and I feel shitty about staying away. My parents are there. I want to spend the holidays with them. But home hasn't been the same since I graduated from high school.

I wish you could come with me to see them. It's been over four years since the last time I saw you. Although your letters make me feel close to you. I think out of all of Knox Ridge, you're the person I miss the most.

Ugh. That's sounds terrible.

I should probably say my parents. They're my biggest supporters. I love them so much. But they're not you. Even if it's just through letters, you're my one stable force. My one constant when the life gets too hard or things don't make sense.

Is it crazy to think that maybe I'm falling for you?

I know we're friends and I shouldn't. There's this pull between us, this feeling. I can't describe it, but we've been this way since we were kids. Now I feel like it's turned into something more. It's strange. Frightening, even.

How can I feel so strongly for someone who isn't even here?

But your letters, the way you entrust everything to me, makes me feel like we could be so much more.

Sorry if this sounds delusional. Maybe I'm just too nostalgic, and whatever this feeling is, will pass. Or maybe one day, this force will take us back to Knox Ridge.

Then maybe this overwhelming feeling will become the biggest love in the universe.

Love,

K

P.S. If I sound crazy, let's never speak of this again.

WHERE THE FUCK has this letter been for the last seven years? I fold it, putting it with the rest of Kaitlynn's letters. After two weeks, I'm finally organizing the stuff my mom left behind for me. I expected old t-shirts and things I'll never use again. But never a few unopened letters from Kaitlynn.

Letters with words I wish I'd been able to tell her years ago.

For years, she's been the one person I wake up thinking of, and the last before I go to sleep. The one I thought of as bullets were flying at close range. Those moments when I thought my life would be over, I wished for one last call, a hug, a kiss.

As Nana said, the stars were filled with wishes of lonely, hopeful people. The entire cosmos could tell the story of how much I wished to see Kit Kat just for one last time. As the years passed, I just couldn't let myself wish for more, or lead her into a life where she could become a widow.

Yet, as contradictory as it sounds, I wish I'd had that letter in my hands all those years ago.

Let's never speak of this again, she'd said.

I slam my forehead with the palm of my hand. She obviously thinks I never had feelings for her. I did...I *do*. And maybe that force that she mentioned is what brought me here. Not Alabama, but Knox Ridge where home is.

The sound of my phone ringing somewhere in the kitchen stops my train of thought. Mom's name flashes on the screen.

"Hey, Mom." I greet her as I pick up the phone.

"Huey," my mom says cheerfully. I bite the growl though. I hate when she uses my middle name. "How are you, pudding?"

"Fine. How are you, Mom?"

"Well if everything's fine, why haven't you taken a minute to call me in the last five days?"

I frown. "I texted you."

She hums. "I didn't know texts were how polite people stay in touch with their mothers. Next thing you're gonna tell me that a Facebook status is a big, old hug."

I roll my eyes. I have to apologize before this guilt trip gets out of hand.

"Sorry, Mama," I lay the accent on really thick, just for her. "I won't let it happen again."

"Glad you found your manners, dear," she says. "So, how's selling the house coming along?"

Selling the house? The last time we talked about the house I clearly told her that I was going to take my time thinking about my next move.

"I...I'm still not sure what I'm going to do, Mom," I admit.

"What does that mean? Toby's expecting you to arrive any day now. A buddy of his owns a men's store where you can buy several suits for work. I already fixed your room up—"

I tune her out as she continues to talk about her husband's plans for me. The man is alright, and I appreciate that he's taking care of Mom. But I don't see myself selling cars…or moving. I can't leave Knox Ridge now. Even more so after reading that letter.

The significance of it is huge. My Katy didn't give up on me… at least not back then.

I know a lot of time has passed. I'm aware that after she sent the letter, she met Steve. But if I would have seen it before, our relationship would be different.

There's something pulling me toward Kaitlynn, and it's not just about wanting to fix the restaurant or her life. It's deeper than that. It's been dormant, but I'm about to wake it up and find out what's really going on between us.

"—Do you want me to call the realtor for you?" Mom says, pulling me out of my thoughts.

"No. Like I said, I don't know what I'm going to do yet," I say.

"What's there to think about?" she asks. "What is in Knox Ridge that you can't find here?"

Kaitlynn, I don't say. *The only home I've ever really known.*

"I'm not sure yet," I say. "But I'll let you know if I find it."

That reminds me of the letters I found. "Hey, I found a few unopened letters. Do you know why I didn't receive them?"

"From Katy," she claims. "They handed them to me while you were in the hospital, hun. I forgot about them. Have you seen her?"

She forgot? That letter was…*is* so important, and she forgot. I exhale harshly. There's no point discussing them with her. I need to talk to Kaitlynn.

"Mom, I have to go."

"Suit yourself," she says reluctantly. "We're ready for you whenever you decide to come home."

After promising to call her tomorrow, we say our goodbyes. As I head out to *Blythe's*, I take a long look at my childhood home. It's a little worse for the wear, but it has some great memories nestled into its cracks. It may not be pretty right now, but it's still worth something to me. It's got some good bones and stories worth telling. Maybe with some time and care, I could make it even better than it once was. *We* could make it a real home.

SEVENTEEN

Kaitlynn

So MUCH FOR my day off. So much more for all those, "Of course I'll be here to help on Monday." Every Sunday, I have a bunch of volunteers who "promise" to show up for Monday Night dinner, and every week, next to no one actually comes.

The dining room is full, and I'm happy about that. All these people deserve a hot meal and a break. But there's only so much I can get done by myself with just two servers. There's a line going out the door.

I'm thankful that I was able to prepare everything before I opened tonight. But I hate to see so many people waiting just because we don't have enough hands to help.

Kelsey's MIA...again. At least she had the decency to text me that she's still alive. I'm hoping she leaves soon. I can't handle the constant uncertainty anymore. If I had the money, I would lend it to her, so she'd leave me alone. Actually, I would use that money to get out of here.

Maybe I should take another look at Javier's offer. His investors turned out to be legitimate. His business partner is pretty successful in the hospitality industry. They could do something with this place...maybe more than I ever have.

My savings account would get its first deposit in years. I could pay off my credit cards. And I could finally be something outside of the confines of this restaurant and the Blythe name.

"Do you need any help?" a husky voice says behind me.

I turn around, glaring at Oliver.

"We're closed today," I say. "You can come back tomorrow."

He takes a long look around the dining room. "You're open. You have customers, and you look swamped. Why would you want me to come back tomorrow when it's obvious that you need me *now*?"

"I don't need *you*," I snap.

"Ok, so you don't need *me*," he says slowly. "But you do need *help*. That's what I'm here for."

Oh, sure. Now he shows up. Where was he when I needed help running this place five years ago? Where was he after my parents died? Or when I poured my heart out in that stupid fucking letter?

"Just leave," I say.

"Kaitlynn, I'm here, what can I do?"

I hate his calm voice and the lack of reaction to my dismissal. We're over. There's nothing left in here for you. I'm drained. I can't give anything else. Just leave me alone.

But what I say is different. "You can't just show up here whenever you feel like it."

"I'm sorry I didn't come yesterday. Striker needed me for a consultation. We didn't come home until earlier today."

I arch an eyebrow and as I'm about to ask, I stop myself. I don't care about his life. He's leaving soon and I have to keep myself guarded at all times. I'm too broken to withstand another hit.

He caresses my cheek with his hand. For a second, I close my eyes, allowing myself to feel comforted. But it's so invasive that I honestly just want to punch him in the gut. I take a step backward, away from him.

"From now on, I promise I'll be here most nights unless I tell you otherwise in advance," he says.

Just get out of here before I get too comfortable around you, I think.

"How about I hire you? You work a few days a week, and I'll know when to expect you," I suggest.

"You can trust me," he says. "I don't see the point of hiring me. I don't need the money."

"Then why are you here?" I ask, but actually I have other questions I want him to answer ...

Why haven't you left yet?

When are you leaving?

...or maybe I want to beg him to stay and...I can't bring myself to believe in him again.

"Because of you," he says softly.

He reaches out his hand again but stops short of touching me. I don't know whether to be grateful or disappointed.

"I would've left Knox Ridge by now if it weren't for you, you know?" he says.

I cross my arms, blushing furiously. "Is that supposed to flatter me?"

"No," he says with a shrug. "I'm just being honest."

Doesn't he know that the last thing I want to hear is someone trash talking Knox Ridge?

"Fuck you. If you knew anything about me, you'd know that's the last thing I want to hear." I glare at him. "How dare you, honestly. How can you turn your back on the town that raised you?"

He takes a step back, crossing his arms. "You left too, Kaitlynn. Don't act all high and mighty with me."

"But I came back," I say.

"So did I! I did it when I was ready," he says.

"What are you saying?"

He assesses me carefully. His eyes scour my soul for something. What? I don't know.

But I have a feeling it died with my parents.

"Sometimes you need to spread your wings and learn about yourself before you put down roots. I didn't come back until I was ready to come home," he says. "Maybe you should have too. You know, that way you wouldn't be stuck resenting a place you 'love' so much."

I grip my arms tighter, frowning. I hate when he makes sense. "You're impossible."

What is he playing at? What's his end goal here?

If I were smart, I would make him either explain himself or else kick him out before he gets too comfortable around here. But I don't know what the fuck to do with him, and I'm drowning trying to get this dinner running smoothly.

I sigh. "Grab an apron and start working. We don't charge on Monday nights."

He raises his eyebrows. "What does that mean?"

"It means don't ask questions and get to work," I say before going back to the kitchen.

EIGHTEEN

Oliver

KAITLYNN'S worse than my superiors back in Iraq. I know she's mad, and it's not only because I wasn't here yesterday.

The best way to cope is by trying to get that long line at the hostess station taken care of, and maybe after closing I can talk to her. Get to the bottom of this.

While working, I find out that Kaitlynn runs a soup kitchen out of this restaurant every Monday. No wonder she's overworked.

When was the last time she took a day off? Can she afford to do this?

I mean, I have no clue what her finances are like, but it can't be cheap to do this every week.

It's not surprising that everyone has something nice to say about Kaitlynn. Her parents were always giving back to the community. Mom and I were lucky to have them.

But she's single-handedly doing more for Knox Ridge than they ever did. The Blythes mainly volunteered around the holidays. Kaitlynn does this year-round.

As I'm coming out of the kitchen, I catch her at one of the back tables, handing over a bag to a family on their way out. I approach the table with the excuse of cleaning, hoping that she's in a better mood.

"Were those leftovers?" I ask.

"No, it was clothes for the kids," she says with a smile.

"Everything's slowing down. Why don't you take a break?"

"Send the other two on a break. I can keep working," she says.

"Do you ever take a break?" I ask.

"Here and there," she responds with a shrug of indifference. "I would rather visit with the customers."

"What you do is amazing, but you need a day off," I tell her.

No wonder she hates this restaurant and town. She's burning herself to the ground.

"Why don't I help you look through the schedule. See if you can take next Sunday off?"

She gives me a tired glare. "I can't afford a day off."

"Then I'll help you with the books," I offer. "We'll find some extra money to pay another server or pay extra to the manager."

"You think it's that simple?"

"Well, it's not as complicated as you're making it," I argue.

"You haven't been here in so long," she says with a huff. "You can't just waltz back in here and assume you know the answer to every problem."

"I don't, but I can try to figure it out for you," I say as I tuck a piece of her hair behind her ear. "Maybe it's time you stop doing everything by yourself, and let someone in."

"I'm sick of trusting people who let me down." She crosses her arms. "What's the point of letting someone in when they'll leave as soon as things get hard?"

"Let me in, Kit Kat," I whisper. "I promise I won't let you down."

Fuck, how long until she trusts me again?

"WHAT ARE YOU DOING HERE?" Kaitlynn asks as I wait for the produce truck to arrive.

I check on the time and say, "I told you to stay in bed. You need some sleep."

"And you don't?"

I shrug. "It's still hard to sleep more than a couple of hours. I'm adjusting. Take advantage of my current situation and relax."

"What's going to happen when you leave?"

"Again, with the leaving," I say exasperated. "When did you stop trusting people?"

She sucks on her bottom lip. "You have to understand that it's been Paige and me for a long time. And I try not to burden her much because she has her own life."

I squeeze her hand and tell her, "you're not alone."

Before she can speak, the produce arrives and right behind him it's the fish guy. While she's checking that everything is in order, I start carrying the crates that she already checked. When we're done, I offer to drive her home.

"What am I supposed to do?"

"Rest. For once in your adult life, take a deep breath and just relax," I advise and leave.

I spend my morning on the phone with the HIB team, discussing the new facilities and the team I'd like to assemble in the south. Bradley understands I won't be able to give him much attention until Blythe's is fully functioning. My family comes first.

By the time I pick up Kaitlynn, I realize this is going to be harder to get her to relax than I thought.

"You baked?"

She shrugs.

"I told you to *relax*."

"Baking relaxes me," she says, eating a spoonful of what looks like blackberry cobbler.

"Give me a couple of days and we'll have a free-kitchen day."

"Now you're being cruel, Oliver," she says, glaring at me.

"Let's go, Katy."

Without another word, she picks up her purse and hands me over two big containers with cookies.

"We have to drive by Paige's. I promise her these cookies."

She reminds me so much of Nana. The way she takes care of everyone, how she works hard and loves harder.

I remember when Nana talked about her late husband, Jonathan Blythe. He was as dutiful, loving and understanding as Richard. A true gentleman.

"That's the kind of man my granddaughters deserve," she used to say. "When you grow up, you'll take care of Katy, Ollie. Just like that."

I don't know if I'll measure up to be like Richard, or Jonathan for that matter. But God help me, I'll try my best to make sure this woman doesn't feel alone again. That she feels cherished and loved.

Last night I told her the truth, I didn't come back until I was ready. Maybe I've loved her since the day I met her, but I hadn't been ready to be the man she deserves until today. Now, the hardest part of the journey is ahead of me, to convince her that I won't let her down ever again.

NINETEEN

Kaitlynn

OLIVER MADE IT HAPPEN. He took a couple of shifts from my manager over the week, so my manager could cover me on Sunday. Actually, he's been working all week, only missing a few hours here and there.

He's doing something on the side. I don't want to ask questions, but what if he's ready to take on a job and leave me behind.

"Relax," he says, as if he could read my thoughts.

Maybe it's not my thoughts but the fact that I'm stiff as a rock and ready to bolt.

Today is our first day off since Monday. Since he wouldn't take the day off unless I agreed not to work. Although I did sneak by the restaurant this morning to receive the catch of the day from my supplier.

Ollie might think that I won't swing by the restaurant all day. But if he thinks I'm skipping closing, he's got another thing coming. No one closes the restaurant but me. I left a procedures list for the staff, but I know they're going to miss something.

He wants me to delegate. He's dead set on becoming part of the *management.* He can't understand why I don't have an accountant...or a business plan. Dad used to handle all of the administrative stuff. My strategy is to follow his procedure—he wrote everything down.

We never budgeted for an accountant. Adding one would kill the minimal profit we currently make. I'd have to start living in the restaurant because I couldn't afford another employee plus my own rent.

Honestly, it's tempting to let Oliver use that business degree he keeps bragging about. But only if I can pay him in something more feasible than cash...like cobbler. I'll throw in a pint of homemade ice cream as his signing bonus. As long as he keeps his hands to himself, I think we'll be fine.

I can't afford crushing on him again. Seven years ago, was bad enough. After he broke my heart, I spent weeks drowning my sorrows in cartons of ice cream and boxes of wine. And that's how I ended up with Steve. "Esteban."

That fucking slimy, comedian weasel. There was nothing funny about him. Once he found out I was leaving for Atlanta, he stole my TV and ran off with my roommate. Not that she was worth it, but her dad was rich, so I guess that counts for something.

"I never got a thank you, you know," I grumble to Oliver who is in the driver's seat next to me.

"For what?"

"Uh, for taking care of your car for the past few years?"

"Hmm...that was you?"

"Who else would do it? Paige kept the plants alive, but do you think she could change the oil by herself?"

"So, you're the reason my car has a lot of extra miles on it?"

I shrug innocently. "Someone had to show this baby what Tybee Island looks like."

"A few hundred times?"

"Maybe." I chuckle.

He laughs. "Well, thanks. I really appreciate it. I should repay you somehow."

"Oh. I don't think that's necessary," I say. "A simple thank you is all I need."

"Nonsense. Let me fix your restaurant for you, and then we'll call it even," he says.

I cross my arms. "You're impossible, Tanner."

"Only because you're stubborn, Blythe," he says.

"I might close it," I confess. Javier's offer is so tempting. "Someone made an offer."

"For what?"

"For the house. Someone wants to buy the restaurant and renovate it. Turn it into a hotel or something," I tell him.

"Are you serious?" he says. "How do you even know this offer is legitimate?"

"Because Javier has the money to back up any crazy idea he comes up with," I explain.

"And you...want to go with a crazy idea? From a guy named Javier? Really?"

"I don't see any better options coming my way," I say. "You've seen the restaurant. There's only so much I can do at this point without going bankrupt."

"So you're going to give it to a stranger? And then what? He guts it dry like any other developer and charges the city a hefty price to let anyone see it?"

I shrug, trying not to care. "It's none of my business what he'd do with it. Hell, his business plan can fail for all I care. If I can't sell this place as a functional restaurant, why not him?"

"I'm giving you the option to fix the place. You're just not letting me do it," he says. "Which brings me to my next question:

do you want to leave Knox Ridge because you're done with the city or just because you're drowning in problems?"

Before I can come up with a reasonable answer, Oliver parks the car. I look out the window, realizing that we're in front of the town arcade. It's been around as long as I've been alive. Ollie and I spent a lot of great afternoons here growing up.

The arcade itself hasn't changed much from the outside, but the owners have made some significant updates to the business by buying a couple of the buildings next to the original arcade.

Now there's laser tag, bowling, and even mini golf. I guess this proves how much I've been out in the last few years. I had no clue this place got a makeover.

Honestly, I wasn't expecting to have fun. If anything, I figured it'd be an awkward waste of a few hours before Ollie let me go home. So, of course, he had to prove me wrong.

The arcade games were exactly how I remembered them. I kicked his ass in mini golf, but he's a soldier so, of course, he owned laser tag. I can't remember the last time I had this much fun.

Somehow, the hours fly right by us. When the announcement that the arcade will be closing in an hour goes off, Ollie invites me back to his place for dinner. Reluctantly, I agree.

His house looks like a museum of ancient artifacts. Nothing's changed, unlike the house next door. The new owners replaced the siding with some weird finish that makes my parent's home look like Arizona threw up in Knox Ridge.

At least, this house still has our memories. I remember when his mom had a day off, they'd invite me over. She'd bake cookies that we'd use for betting during card games. I'd usually wipe the floor with Ollie. He was always too open as a kid. I could tell what he was thinking just by glancing at his face.

"I think I'll fix this house too," he says with an unreadable expression as we get out of his car.

I sigh. Ollie used to make sense. *We* used to make sense. Those were the days.

TWENTY

Kaitlynn

As Carl, the contractor, leaves the restaurant, I feel a headache coming on after hearing his fucking quote. It's going to be ten thousand more than I expected, plus appliances.

I stopped him before he started running numbers on the outdoor patio idea. There's no way I can afford it on top of all the renovations this place needs.

That's it. I'm moving to LA.

"What's with that face?" Oliver says as he comes inside.

He's carrying a toolbox in one hand and a can of paint in the other.

"What's with the paint?" I ask.

"Before you open for dinner, I want to fix a few things, at least in the back. Then we can talk about renovating the rest."

Without a word, I hand him the quote Carl just gave me. He takes the sheet, eyes widening to comical proportions.

"And that's just the interior," I tell him dryly. "The price tag doesn't include appliances, decorations, or tableware."

He whistles. "Well, that's one opinion."

"He's the best contractor in town, and he gave me a great discount," I say. "I'm not going to get a better price than this."

"What if I told you that I could do the initial repairs for free, and loan you the money to cover the rest of the renovation?"

"And next you're going to offer to build a new patio for outside," I say sarcastically. "Should I pinch myself now, or do you want to wake me up yourself?"

He opens his mouth to say something, but I interrupt him.

"You know what? Don't. Just tell me, could you even afford to do all of that?" I point at the paper he holds.

"Yeah, of course. The patio will be included," he says. "I've been working for twelve years, and I haven't spent much of it yet. The savings add up."

I stare at him. My mind is blown. I thought he was just talking a big game. But this could honestly work. Then again...once this is over, he's going to leave for Montgomery—with his mom.

He's going to be expecting his money back, probably with interest, and I'm going to be alone. I'll still be stuck here, begging people to work at this restaurant like always.

I don't feel like wasting another five years of my life when I could just cut my losses now.

"Thanks, but uh, no thanks," I say.

"Isn't this what you need? Just to fix this restaurant to stay?"

"Like I told you, I need a lot more than that," I say. "I need someone to work with me. I can't keep doing this by myself. I need people who can support me and help keep this place sustainable. Not someone who comes in for five seconds with a charity act and then leaves as soon as their savior complex tells them they did a 'job well done.'"

"You won't have to," he says. "I'll be here."

"Just until the reno is done. Then you'll be going to your family."

"I'm not going anywhere," he says firmly. "As long as you're still in Knox Ridge, I'll be here."

"So, if I stay here for a hundred years, you're not moving away?"

"Yep," he says. "It's time that we finally got on the same page."

I glare at him. Is he implying that he wants us to be together?

Am I making shit up again in my head like I did in high school? Or in college for that matter.

Yep, it's the latter. Just be firm, keep your heart safe and Oliver away.

Why am I always putting myself in this stupid situation where I wait around for him to catch feelings that he'll never have? I should put a stop to this before I get attached. Before he starts bringing a blonde bombshell around, and I end up drinking myself stupid at my own fucking bar.

"What if I promise to think about it? Is that enough?" I offer.

"What's there to think about?" he gives me a challenging glare.

"I could just sell this restaurant and move to LA or back to Atlanta," I argue. "I'd be selling the building for more than the restaurant is worth. Then I wouldn't owe you. I could pay off the bank, and I could start over with a clean slate."

"Give me a chance," he insists. "If it doesn't work out, you can still sell it. It'll be worth more after we fix it up."

I take a deep breath. He's really not giving up on this. It's better to just let him try and fail, I think, than to keep arguing.

"Ok," I say finally. "Let's go with your plan. Even though I know I'm going to end up selling."

"HOW DID you convince me to close up this place for an entire week?"

"I'm still asking myself the same question," Oliver says with a triumphant grin.

We just finished painting the dining room a calm sage color. Tomorrow we're ripping out the carpet and seeing what's underneath. The old hardwood might be in decent condition, at least that's what Oliver said. He's probably right. It's probably cheaper to buff out a few scratches in wood and stain it than to replace the carpet with something less ugly.

He's been right all over the place these last couple of weeks. He's wearing me down. Every morning he brings coffee and cupcakes or muffins from Paige's bakery. He works in the kitchen before I start prepping for the day, and then he goes to the back office to mess with the books. Even the customers are noticing little changes.

I both love and hate that things are working out as well as they are. Is it crazy to be on high alert, waiting for the other shoe to drop? It's been so long since my life hasn't been just a sequence of kitchen disasters and employee meltdowns. Oliver's presence has made a huge difference.

Every day something changes around here—even me. The only thing that I hate is when I get jealous. Every time he's in the dining room and some young single customer is eyeing him like a piece of meat, I get so angry. Angry at them for looking at him that way, and angry at myself for caring. So much for keeping my distance.

But how can I? When he calls me beautiful every day, checks up on me during shifts, and acts like my problems actually matter. I wanted to stay safe. But some days, he makes me want more.

Passion, excitement...comfort.

Feelings that can only come from being wrapped up in the arms of a man like him.

I like that we can spend the entire day doing nothing, working amicably in silence, while still having the time of our lives. When he's around, I can't catch my breath. It's like I come alive whenever I'm near him.

I'm being incredibly naïve here, which is dangerous. He's like my oxygen at this point, just like he used to be.

What am I going to do when he leaves?

"Are you ok?" he asks.

"For now," I say honestly. "So, what does your mom think about you hanging around here? Doesn't she miss you?"

He shrugs. "Sure. She's hoping that I'll move in with her."

I nod, humming absentmindedly. Maybe he'll take the hint and start working on his exit strategy.

Of course, he has to be stubborn and say, "You have to understand that I'm not moving, unless you leave."

"So, if I move to Atlanta?" I ask critically.

"It's only four hours from Montgomery, we can visit her often," he replies.

"How about LA?"

"Then I guess we're moving to LA and she'll have to fly over to visit us," he says casually.

"Why would you move to LA?" My voice trembles as he walks closer to me.

"I'd go wherever you are. That's," he kisses my forehead, "why," he kisses my nose, "I'm here."

His piercing eyes stare at me for several beats before he speaks again. "For you."

The world stops as he leans in slowly, his gaze never leaving mine. My heart flips eagerly, my entire body tingles as the anticipation increases until he slams his lips to mine nearly knocking the wind from my lungs. Yet, I feel alive.

He presses his tongue to the seam of my lips and, at my acquiescence, delves into my mouth. My arms reach up and tangle around his thick, strong neck. He pulls me up to his broad chest. I moan as his body heat burns mine through our clothing. His hands drift to my hips, settling there while our tongues swirl together. Oliver devours me, like he's been starving.

"Come home with me." He breaks the kiss, nuzzling my neck.

"I don't think—"

"No, Kit Kat," he whispers. "Let me take care of you. Be with you."

I should push him away, but the fire in his soul numbs the logical side of my mind. In no time, we're out of the restaurant and in his car heading to his house. We remain silent the five minutes it takes to drive home.

"We could've stayed in the restaurant," I protest when we enter his room.

"I don't want to push you," he stops in the middle of his room, looking at me. "We don't have to do anything."

"This will complicate everything." I sober up from the passionate kiss we shared at the restaurant.

"Our being together isn't a complication." He takes a step closer. "Our relationship is casual. No…the word I'm looking for is *simple*."

Simple, I repeat to myself. No strings attached.

He takes me by the waist, his loving eyes look at me with such tenderness I can't remember why we shouldn't be in his room. Instead, I raise the hem of his shirt lifting it up his torso. His arms lift, going over his shoulders as he yanks his shirt over his head. I stare at his chiseled torso while his fingers fidget with my clothing. *This is crazy*, a voice in my head whispers. But I let him, and the passion that's been burning inside me since the moment he came back to town, lead me.

Oliver's head angles slightly to the side as his lips come closer to mine. My mouth parts as his brushes against it. Our breaths mingle, along with our tongues. My heart flutters as his arms encircle my warm body. This wasn't our first kiss, but it obliterated every thought.

For the first time, my mind is locked into the moment, locked into us. His body so close to mine, his hands slowly peeling away my clothes. I wish the kiss would never end.

The intensity of our kiss rises. It's raw, and my heartbeat intensifies as his hands touch my bare skin. It's been too long since someone has touched me, longer even that I've been wanting *his* touch. As his fingers brush my soft flesh, my hands slide upwards across his hard chest.

"Are you sure about this?" he asks, as he pushes me closer to his bed.

I stare at him for a few moments, fighting my conscience.

This is wrong, because you're feeling things for him that he'll never feel for you, says one voice.

Do it. You finally get to live your fantasy, says the other one.

It was a fantasy when I was younger. Today it's the pent-up energy accumulated from watching him working in the restaurant. How he casually caresses my hand as we exchange trays, or glances at me from across the room. The sweet smiles, the soft words while we're having lunch.

Oliver is the first person who's cared for me since my parents died. No one has eaten my food with the enthusiasm he does.

I don't answer with words, but with a kiss. A kiss where I claim him. It's desperate, wild. A second later I'm on my back. Oliver unzips my jeans and tugs them down along with my panties. Then I feel his finger filling me as his mouth feathers kisses along my knees, trailing up toward my torso, nibbling every inch of my skin until he's sucking on my nipple.

He teases my breasts, sucking them, flicking them, taking me to the edge, while his long finger continues to thrust in and out of my entrance.

"Oliver," I moan, pushing myself into his hand, my back arching as I seek relief.

"You're wet, and ready," he says huskily.

Suddenly, he pushes himself off the bed, and he's fishing for a condom inside his wallet before pulling down his pants. My mouth waters as I take in all of him. He's beautiful. As astonishing as Michelangelo's David. He's hard, as if his skin were made of marble, and it knocks my breath right out of me.

He opens my legs, rolls the condom along his thick, long length, and climbs into bed next to me. He takes a long glance at my body, and the gesture feels like a caress through my soul.

"You're beautiful," he says as he pushes my knees farther apart and kneels right in front of me.

His hand wraps around his dick, and he lowers himself, resting the head right at my entrance. His mouth captures mine as he pushes himself inside me, filling me inch by inch.

God, it feels so good.

In an instant, we become a tangle of bodies, arms, and mouths driving deep into each other. Fast. Hard.

Oliver cups my breast, playing with my nipples. My hips meet his as he keeps thrusting inside me as if he's trying to fuse our two bodies. I open myself to the possibilities. I open my heart to him as his kiss intensifies. He grips me into a desperate clutch, holding me tight against his rapid thrusts. My channel squeezes him as ripples of pleasure pulse through me, igniting every cell of my body. I explode, breaking into a million pieces and becoming dust.

I dig my nails into his back as he goes rigid on my arms, whispering my name. "Kit Kat."

My name on his lips sounds like a prayer, an oath. I cling to him for several breaths. His face is buried in the crook of my shoulder. I savor this moment. Save it in case it's the only one like this we ever share.

Chapter Twenty-One

K<small>IT</small> K<small>AT</small>,

Death isn't kind. It just takes people away. It doesn't care who you are, what you've done, or who will miss you when you're gone. It just rips people apart.

Today, I almost left. I don't fear death. I fear leaving you behind. I fear not telling you how I feel about you. How I have felt all these years. You're the only thing I think about when we're out scouting. You're the one thing that gets me to sleep at night. You're the most important person in my life, and the worst part about being out here is knowing that I might never see you again.

I'm not exactly sure when I fell for you. But I know I have feelings, and they burn stronger every day. Your letters are what keep me alive in this sea of bullets, blood, and sand.

Mine isn't a fairytale. Maybe a morose story with a bittersweet ending. Though I pray that someday I can see your beautiful face again. Some days that feels like an impossible fever dream.

I wish I were home with you right now, or that I was brave enough to send you this letter.

Always Yours,
Oliver

OLLIE,

Hey, it's been a while. Why haven't you written back? Are you alright? I miss you.

Enjoy everything I sent you, and I hope I gave you enough to share.

Kaitlynn

OLIVER,

You still haven't written back. At this point, I'm not sure whether to be annoyed or upset. If it's about the letter I sent you, like I said just forget about it. If that's really why you aren't talking to me, we can move past it.

I miss you, ok? I don't know how many times to say it or how to say it right. You're my best friend, and you're on the other side of the world. Some days I can't stand it. I know you're out there doing things for the greater good and world peace or whatever, but I'd rather have you at home.

I don't even know if you're safe or not because you won't talk to me. You can't freeze me out like this, Ollie. We've been through too much for you to do that.

Can't you at least give me a sign? Say just a simple "fuck off" so I'll at least know you're alive? Is that too much to fucking ask?

Kaitlynn

OLIVER,

You know what this reminds me of? That time you almost kissed me. You were seventeen and I was sixteen, we were in the backyard of your mom's house. I was watching the sunset and you hadn't seen me. It was the perfect moment after the perfect day. We had spent the perfect summer together.

I thought we were perfect.

You leaned over, and I closed my eyes. I waited and waited.

Your mom interrupted, and you never tried again.

We were so close, I thought it meant something to you.

That I meant something to you.

I had fallen for my best friend. Just like my parents had fallen years ago. It was the beginning of my own fairy tale.

—it wasn't.

Nana almost said that perfection is just an illusion. She's so right.

It only took you two weeks to move on, though. You started dating Kelsey. I had to watch you two kiss and makeout right in front of me. It was humiliating, you know that?

It's almost the same.

As soon as you left, and we started exchanging letters. I felt close to you again. It's like those years apart didn't matter. Nothing mattered because I had you...I thought I had you.

My mistake.

I guess I was just reading between the lines. You're a good friend, maybe I've always mistaken that for something more...You were a good friend, I thought.

But good friends don't date their friend's sisters like you did, and good friends don't read what I told you in the letter and then shove you out of their life.

I think you're a good person, Ollie, and you might be a really great guy. But I can't keep being your friend anymore if this is how you're going to treat me. I deserve better than this.

Kaitlynn

TWENTY-TWO

Oliver

MY BED IS EMPTY. I look around, and Kaitlynn is nowhere to be found. Fuck, I knew she was skittish about tonight. But she promised to stay the night. I groan, reaching out blindly for the shirt I had on earlier. Instead of finding it, I grab ahold of what feels like Kaitlynn's bra.

At least she's still here. I stumble through the darkness, flipping on the light switch so I can put some underwear on. I decide to head downstairs to see if I can find her.

From the top of the stairs, I hear some muffled sound coming from downstairs. I creep down cautiously, relaxing when I see that it's Kaitlynn sitting on the couch...with one of the boxes my mom left for me wide open.

She's clutching a piece of paper in one hand and covering her mouth with the other. Shit, what did I do this time?

"What's wrong?" I ask quietly.

"You almost died," she says. "You never told me that."

What the fuck. "Why did you open those letters? They were closed. I haven't even read them."

"Well why didn't you open them before? You had them for *eight fucking years*," she argues.

"I never got them," I say.

"And they just...magically appeared in this fucking box?"

"Mom received them while I was in the hospital," I say. "She was by my side the entire time."

"So that's why you stopped writing? You were hurt," she says quietly. "Are these all the letters?"

Does she want to know where the other letter is? It's on my nightstand. I must have read it a thousand times since I first opened it a few weeks ago. I don't know if I'm ready for her to see that—or for us to discuss it.

"I have all of them," I say casually.

She nods, clenching the letter tightly in her hands. Great, she's fucking up the paper. I sit down next to her, gently pulling the sheets away from her. I can't have her ruining these. They aren't as important as her, but they matter.

Kaitlynn looks up from her lap, staring at me intensely. I can't tell whether she wants to cry some more or punch me. Maybe it's both.

I don't know what to do or what's going on in her head. Her gears look like they're grinding really hard as her eyes glaze over. I stand up, shuffling away awkwardly.

"Why don't I get you something to drink?" I offer, walking toward the kitchen. "Coffee?"

"You have anything stronger?" she asks.

"Uh, I'll see what I can do," I tell her.

This house has been emptied for a decade. I don't know what she's expecting. I search through the pantry, checking if there's any leftover liquor that my mom forgot to take with her, when Kaitlynn comes bustling into the kitchen.

Her movements are fucking mechanical as she searches through the cabinets. She still knows where everything is, apparently, grabbing baking utensils from various spots. I sigh, taking a seat at the kitchen table as she does...whatever it is she's doing.

"Where did I leave the honey," she mutters.

I blink. "What?"

She doesn't answer me. A minute or two later, she finds the honey she was talking about, and it looks edible.

When was the last time she was in here?

Watching her work is like watching an orchestra play in the middle of an action movie. I'm not sure if it's beautiful or terrifying, and I can't tell what exactly I'm supposed to be focusing on. But somehow, she pulls together honey biscuits like it's nothing.

After she sets them in the oven, I notice her hands trembling. She sits down quietly across from me, her arms crossed close to her chest. Kaitlynn is...still a little terrifying to me.

I clear my throat. "So…"

"You can't just fucking die and not tell me about it," her voice is tight and panicked.

"I didn't die," I remind her.

"And how the fuck was I supposed to know that?" she snaps. "You weren't dead, but you wouldn't fucking answer...and then you did almost die and you still couldn't fucking say 'hey, I'm still alive?'"

"I was in the hospital, and then—"

"And then you were at another site, and you got your promotion, and every fucking thing came before Kaitlynn," she says. "I get it."

"I didn't say that," I argue.

She shrugs. "You might as well have."

I take a deep breath. "Look, I'm sorry I didn't tell you. But that's in the past. I'm here now and—"

She groans. "Yes, now. You're here now. Not last year when I could've salvaged this restaurant. Not five years ago when I needed you."

What does she want me to say?

I wish I had been with her. I've missed her every single day for the last twelve years. Even now when she's sitting right in front of me, I miss her. I miss the way she was, and the people we were. I like this Kaitlynn, and I'm falling in love with her...but I loved my Kit Kat.

"I'm sorry," I say, still at a loss for words.

Kaitlynn shakes her head, pushing her seat away from the table and slowly getting up.

"You don't get it," she fumes. "I mean...fuck, I guess at some point you might've understood. But too little, too late, I guess."

"What does that mean?"

She takes a deep breath. "Why don't you take a look at those letters you didn't read? Then tell me you're sorry."

She trudges out of the kitchen. Her footsteps are heavy and slow against the staircase. I listen intently until I hear the quiet thud of my bedroom door shutting. I run a hand through my hair.

Eventually, I muster up the energy to look through those fucking letters. I grab the second one in the pile since it's mostly unwrinkled. I start to read it, and my stomach drops.

Oliver, it reads. *You know what this reminds me of? That time you almost kissed me.*

TWENTY-THREE

Kaitlynn

OLLIE ENTERS HIS ROOM, sitting next to me on his unmade bed. He kisses the tears from my cheeks, and I feel his lips against mine. He sweeps my hair aside, kissing my neck. Nibbling my ear.

"I'm sorry," he murmurs as his arms encircle my body.

Stupidly, I sink myself into his arms, letting him comfort me. Everything I feared while he was away almost happened. The loneliness is choking me, squeezing my lungs while I realize that I've had no one in my life.

Not even after my parents died, and I'm *still* here waiting for someone to be by my side. From the beginning I knew it'd happen.

I'd fall back in love.

"I was a stupid kid," he mumbles. "God, if I had known…"

Closing my eyes, I wait for more.

He says nothing for several beats. His mouth rests on my shoulder, his voice is low. It caresses my skin, making it tremble as he speaks. "But for so long I've been an idiot who had no idea how to care for a treasure like you."

"Ollie," I sob against his chest.

He shifts his head to the right and kisses me. One hand at the back of my neck. Our mouths move against each other. It's a soft kiss.

The tenderness pieces back together the broken shards of my heart. Even when it's slow, the way his tongue slides against mine ignites a fire. His big, rough hands slide up and down my body, pulling my shirt over my head, throwing it to the floor.

His mouth moves down my throat, his hands tangle in my hair. The heat that's radiating from his body is burning every part of mine.

I want more than his caresses.

I need everything.

I want him to fill me—to complete me.

To remind me that he's alive. He's here with me. At least for the rest of the night.

Releasing my hair, his lips trail over my skin. He places tender kisses on my collar bone and my breasts. His fingers skate down my spine, circling my hips and down my thighs. That mouth that's awakening every inch of my body follows right behind his hands.

Oliver pushes my legs apart, his digits brushing against my folds, making me squirm as he moves them up and down before opening my entrance. He places his mouth right on my core. His breath sends a ripple of pleasure from my sensitive lips to my body.

I close my eyes when his flat tongue presses against my clit, and I release a soft moan. My hands clench into fists, grabbing onto his soft hair. Inserting one long finger into my channel, he fucks me with his hand and his mouth.

My hips rock against his face, demanding more, for the ache to disappear, for him to make everything better. I'm so close to the edge, about to fall, when he stops.

His dark eyes are oceans of lust and desire. "I want to be inside you," he says, narrowing his gaze. "But I don't have any condoms."

"I'm clean and on the pill," I say, not wanting to wait. "Are you?"

"Clean?" He nods. "I've always used protection."

Without another word, I'm on my back and he's on top of me, his cock pushing past my entrance, filling up my pussy. He stills for a couple of breaths, and my pussy clenches as I feel him throbbing inside me.

"You're perfect," his breathless words come out as a prayer.

Then, he kisses me as he pushes himself deeper, so deep I become an extension of him. My throat releases a guttural moan. I expect him to thrust in and out of me wildly, but instead, he takes his time rolling his hips as he pulls out gently and enters me tenderly. I feel loved, worshiped with every movement.

Tonight, I surrender completely to the moment. To him. I let my dream become the reality I've wished for so many years. Drunk with passion and love, I climax, crying Oliver's name as he fills me with his seed, and in doing so, fulfills my fantasy.

His lips move against mine, then he kisses the top of my head and my ear murmuring words I can't understand and for one second, I think he says, *I love you*. But my eyes are so heavy, I disregard his musings and just let myself fall asleep in his arms. At least for one night.

IT'S a little after sunrise when I wake up. My head is pounding like a twelve-ton bulldozer just ran over it. It's probably from dehydration or that I'm not used to sleeping this much. There's a soft snore next to me.

I glance at Oliver, taking him in like a picture I can't keep. My hand trembles, hovering over his head. If I could just fix his hair, pretend this was just like old times—that would be perfect.

But it isn't. Ollie's lying fucking naked next to me. He looks so good like this, warm and calm against the sheets. This is the one thing I always dreamed of having, aside from my own TV show.

I take a deep breath, forcing myself out of bed. I slip my clothes on, grabbing my phone off the nightstand. There's so much to do today, and I'm already behind schedule. I creep down the stairs quietly. It's been awhile, but I know how to avoid every creaky floorboard in this place.

The cicadas are shrieking in the distance, reminding me that this isn't a dream. I guess I don't have to pinch myself to see if I'm dreaming. Their cries are just as loud as the pain in my chest. Everything feels tight, too tight.

The fridge hums as I tiptoe past the kitchen. I'll have to come back later to wash the dishes. It's not like this is the first time I've left them there for a day or two before returning. There's only so much of this house I can take at one time.

It's pure and inviting because of how much time I spent here as a kid. When the restaurant was too busy, or the house was too quiet, the Tanner's house was my home away from home.

Since Josey designated me to check on the house periodically, sometimes, I feel like this is my house more than my apartment. I sigh, slipping my shoes on before walking out the front door, locking it as I leave with my spare key.

What will happen when a new family moves in?

There'll be no place for me to hide when I need to feel close to home.

The shitty thing about leaving home, is that it's never the same once you leave. In some ways, it stops being the place to land when things get hard. It constantly shifts. Stray for too long and the ground disappears underneath you, leaving behind only a memory of what used to be.

That's the problem with Ollie's house, and all of Knox Ridge, for that matter.

Blythe's isn't too far from here. I can get there in maybe fifteen minutes if I walk at a fast pace. The farther I get from Oliver, the more reality washes over me. Things become clearer.

What we shared last night was good...too good to be true, honestly.

I shiver, wishing I'd brought my sweater with me from last night, or stolen one of Ollie's old hoodies from his closet.

But that would've caused a commotion, and probably woken him. I had to get out of there as fast as I could. There's no use waking him up and dealing with the fall out of what will be the most awkward let down in history.

Oliver is a sweet guy. He really tries to be there for other people. But this was too much. He can't just offer a pity fuck and hope that smooths everything over.

That's all it was, anyway. He's always got to fix things for everyone, even when he doesn't have all the answers. He just jumped headfirst into the best solution he could think of to make me less miserable.

I should appreciate it. But as my stomach twists itself in knots, I have to clutch myself tighter. I'm trying to keep it together long enough to get inside of the restaurant. The air is still brisk, slinking its way down my throat painfully like icy shards.

An apology and a pity fuck aren't what I need. I needed closure. I needed Ollie to say that we were never going to be like that, and that he's sorry for leading me on. I can't deal with being halfway in between something and nothing for years on end.

Not anymore.

That was the only solace I had while we weren't talking—that he couldn't hurt me if we didn't have contact. I want to hate him for making me feel as if I mattered—as if he loved me.

The stairs into Blythe's are short and not steep, but this morning the feat feels harder than climbing Mount Everest. I fumble with the keys as I unlock the front door. I glance at the clock on the wall. The delivery guy should be here any minute.

I scrub my face, heading toward the bathroom to splash some water on me. When I stare at myself in the mirror—wet, cold, and with purple bags under my eyes—I feel like screaming.

When did my life become a series of one bad decision after another?

When did happiness become a vague fairytale instead of a regular fucking emotion?

I can't stand to look at myself any longer and head toward the bar.

This isn't the face of someone who's living, but rather just coasting, existing. I thought my rock bottom was when I stopped being able to afford my own groceries. I never thought it could get worse.

My phone buzzes in my back pocket. The delivery guy is running late this morning. I slump against the bar. Just perfect. I can't get a guy. I can't keep up with a restaurant or my sister. I can't even get fucking fish here on time.

"I think it's time to call it quits," I say out loud to no one.

I'll start looking up the number of a local realtor in a minute. But first, I flip through the contacts on my phone. It rings for a few seconds before someone on the other line picks up.

"Javier?" I say. "It's Kaitlynn. If the offer's still open, I'd love to take it."

We talk about setting up a meeting with our realtors and the kind of timeline I should expect for this to go through.

After I hang up with him, I call the realtor leaving her a message and promising to send a detailed email in a couple of hours. The last call is harder, but I have to make it for my own good.

"Do you know what time it is?" Kelsey's groggy and snappy voice answers.

Time for me to take control of my life.

"I wanted to let you know that I'm selling Blythe's," I inform her, glancing at the restaurant one last time.

Remembering Mom and Dad has me almost in tears because Javier and his investors won't care about their fights, their kisses, or the way they taught me how to prepare the best peach cobbler in all of Knox Ridge.

"Well, send me my cut when you have the cash."

"Your cut?" I huff. "I paid you more than what this restaurant was worth. Whatever I get from it will be mine."

"That's not fair."

"What's not fair is running the place to the ground when it was one of the best restaurants in Knox Ridge. What's not fair is selling our family home without giving me a cent…your attitude isn't fair. I needed you when they died, and you only appeared after I had already taken care of everything. I'm done with you, Kelsey."

"Well, I'm done with you too. I went to fucking Knox Ridge to help you and you didn't pay me."

"You never helped me. Not this season, or ever. You always take what's not yours, break it and dispose of it as if it never mattered," I remind her, my voice echoing through the empty restaurant. "Until you grow up and realize that I'm your sister, don't bother talking to me."

"Is this because you're sleeping with my ex?"

"What are you talking about?"

"There's a rumor going around that you hired Oliver and now you're fucking him. Which is kind of disgusting. He was mine."

"We're not together. But if we were, it's not any of your damn business. You two broke up years ago, and you're a married woman."

"Ah, little Katy is still pining for him. He chose me over you—just remember that."

"Grow the fuck up, Kelsey. He didn't choose you. You trapped him because he was convenient, and he was a stupid kid. When you decide to be a real Blythe, give me a call."

I hang up, locking the restaurant and driving away toward my new life.

TWENTY-FOUR

Oliver

WHERE IS SHE? Kaitlynn isn't answering my calls. I've been looking for her since the moment I woke up. She wasn't at my house. She wasn't at her apartment. The restaurant is empty. The fish is outside, which is so unlike her.

Ollie: *Where are you? I'm putting the fish in the freezer. Call me. We need to talk.*

She doesn't answer my text, so I start ripping up the carpet like we planned. The floor is in almost perfect condition. It just needs to be sanded and polished.

Hopefully, I can convince her to close on Monday too. I understand the soup kitchen is important to her. But with that extra day, I should be able to finish with the floors, and then we can buy new furniture.

Would she let me be her business partner if I asked?

Would that be too much to ask?

I'll put down enough money to get this business into a healthy start. A clean slate that will allow her to do what she wants with her life and pursue her dreams.

Perhaps we should start by discussing what happened yesterday. I'm not one to talk about feelings, but I want her to know that I love her.

All these years, I've been such an idiot. I dated Kelsey, when I should've dated Kaitlynn. I was too scared of losing Kaitlynn to give us a real shot. It was safer to remain friends.

While I was in the service, I should have reached out to her. There were times when I was tempted to visit her. But I didn't see the point. At least, I didn't see it then. Now I regret all the opportunities I missed out on by being a coward.

Oliver: *It's two o'clock. Where the fuck are you? I'm worried.*

Kaitlynn: *Talking with my realtor. We're meeting with Javier next week and there's a lot of shit left to fix before he gives us a decent price.*

What the fuck?

She gave up on us, just like that. I thought things were improving. I glance around the restaurant. We've been working so hard on this place, and each other, or so I thought. We were so close.

Why is she giving up like that?

I exhale harshly before calling her. The phone rings for so long that I assume she's sending me to voicemail. But finally, she does pick up.

"Hey," she says.

"You're kidding, right?" I ask. "You're fucking with me. Tell me it was a joke and you're in your apartment getting ready and on your way over right now."

"Uh, no," she says. "I'm on the other side of town. We're getting ready a to-do list that I have to work on during the next week or so. Blythe's is officially closed."

"What the literal fuck, Kaitlynn? You have a restaurant. You have responsibilities, and people who depend on you. You can't just drop everything and give up."

"I'm selling the restaurant," she says curtly. "Javier will do what he wants, and the town will move on just like it always does."

"What about the people who count on their Monday meal?"

"If I stay in Knox Ridge, I won't have enough to feed them in a month or two," she says. "Or myself, for that matter."

I hear her make a sound that's sort of like a muffled sob.

"I need to start taking care of Kaitlynn," she says. "You know?"

"That's what I'm here for. That's what I was trying to do," I insist.

"I need a more permanent solution, but I appreciate your kindness."

"What about us?" I ask desperately.

"There is no us," she says. "There's never been an 'us'. We aren't anything, Ollie. Just a couple of strangers who ran into each other again. Like ships passing in the night."

Before I can argue, she hangs up.

I try to call her again, but the call goes directly to voicemail. Instead of leaving, I stay in the restaurant, sanding the floors. I still can't believe she did this.

I tried to fix the building. I tried to keep her restaurant up and running. I tried to be her friend first. I thought we were getting somewhere.

I thought she saw the same potential that I saw in this place.

In us.

I keep pushing the sander, letting the vibrations numb my hands since it can't numb my heart.

What did she mean by saying we aren't anything?

She's the one writing fucking letters about how there's a pull between us, and we're destined for each other and all of that shit. She wasn't making that up. I know Kaitlynn.

So really, the question is, why is she so insistent on lying to herself?

She talks about Knox Ridge likes it's horrible, but I know she loves it. She loves this place and everything about it. I sigh, wiping the sweat from my brow. I take a long look around the dining room. It looks decent enough.

Fuck, I worked all day and it feels like I got nothing done. The renovations aren't finished, and the new appliances arrive next week. I wonder if this is what her life's been like, working hard by herself to get next to nowhere.

I take a deep breath as I unplug the sander. It's been five years since her parents died. Her sister's never around...she has what? One friend?

Her staff is a revolving door, and she can barely keep this place open. I knew her finances weren't great, but the way she was talking about them earlier...

The more I think about it, the more I can't imagine how she kept all this going for so long. When she talks about the restaurant, she sounds like some of my veteran buddies—worn out, jaded, and disillusioned about why she even did this in the first place.

Feeling as if this will never end and when it does, she'll be alone. She has me, how do I convince her that I'm not the same boy who couldn't keep his shit together and ran away from her?

On my way home, I think more about our future. I don't know what I'm going to do, but I don't want to quit. I won't quit. She fought my battles when we were kids against my will.

This time I'll be doing the same. Fight her battles, stand next to her, and show her she matters.

That I'm hers.

That we belong to each other.

Now that I've had her, I can't imagine my life without her. As I pass the old movie theatre, I remember that I haven't called my mom in two days. I better do it now before she has my neck.

"Hi, Huey," she says as she picks up on the third ring. "How are you, hun?"

"I'm fine," I lie.

"I can smell the horse shit from here, sweetheart," she says. "Now why don't you tell me what's wrong?"

"She's selling the restaurant. She wants to get the hell out of here," I tell her.

"Oh," she says. "So, when are you moving?"

"Moving where?"

"To wherever she's going...that is what you called tell me, right?" she says slowly. "That you're moving away with your girlfriend."

"No, Mom. She's not my girlfriend."

"Well, why not? That's what everyone's been talking about for the last three weeks."

"Everyone?"

"Dear, really," she says. "You think you've been discreet with all that flirting you've been doing around Blythe's? You think a friend just offers to fix up his friend's restaurant and then invites her over to his place?"

"How do you know about that?"

"I still Skype in for my knitting circle," she says primly.

"Why I am not surprised?" I say with a sigh.

"Close your mouth, dear," she says. "I know the look you're giving me. I have to say, if you aren't dating her and she's leaving, what the hell are you still doing in Knox Ridge?"

"I need to finish renovating the house..."

"The house you haven't started yet because you've been making googly eyes at Kaitlynn Blythe?"

I groan. "What's your point?"

"It's okay to miss living there, sweetie. Lord knows that was the only home and only family you ever loved."

"That's not true."

"Oh it is," she says. "But don't worry, I'm a part of it so I don't feel too bad about you being a Knox Ridge boy. Your father always said there was something special about living there. He said 'once you get a whiff of that air and your toes in the grass, it's like your soul plants roots down there. It's always a part of you just like you're a part of it.'"

I swallow back feeling of loneliness I haven't felt in years. "Why'd you leave? Really, what was it?"

She sighs. "You're not the only one with skeletons there, Huey. At some point...I got sick of burying my friends and loved ones. It will always be my home, but I can't make myself stay somewhere that no longer gives me joy. In Montgomery, I have Toby. We've built a life together and I'm happy."

"I'm sorry," I say. "I didn't mean—"

"Relax," she says calmly. "I'm happy now and that's what matters. Now it's time for you to get happy too. So, get off your cute little heinie and go get your girl back."

"But—"

"No buts, Oliver Hugh Tanner," she says. "I kept quiet when you blew it with her the first time. You should have never dated that spray tan she calls a sister. I won't let you spoil things for yourself again."

Well, I can't argue with that.

As if reading my mind, she says, "Huey, if I sound stern, it's only because I want what's best for you. And I have never seen anyone, or anything make you as happy as Katy does. So why in God's name are you standing in your own way again?"

"You're right," I say.

"I know," she says matter-of-factly. "I'm always right. Call me when you've figured things out with her."

She hangs up before I can argue with her. Dammit, what's with women and hanging up on me like that?

What can I say to convince Kaitlynn to come back, when everything I tried to do for her wasn't enough?

Actually...what if I'm not enough?

This is too big for just one person and we don't have enough time to save it.

I start making calls to different people in town, finally realizing this problem is much bigger than me.

TWENTY-FIVE

Kaitlynn

AFTER FIGHTING on the phone with Ollie, I don't know what I'm doing anymore. Not because I've suddenly been filled with this love and passion for the restaurant again...it's something else.

My gut twists during the entire meeting with my realtor.

Carolyn Smith took over the family business a year ago, her mom started selling houses in town thirty-five years ago. She looked at me like I was crazy when I first arrived. But the more I explained, the more she understood.

As she ushers me toward the door, promising to follow up on some things tonight, she gives me a sympathetic nudge.

"We'll get this squared away really fast, alright?" Carolyn says. "You won't have to worry about it for much longer."

I nod somberly. "Thanks, I really appreciate it."

She bites her lip. "Can I give you a hug?"

That takes me completely by surprise, but I nod. "Sure."

She hugs me tightly. Fuck, I always forget how long it's been since someone's hugged me until I'm about to cry in someone's arms.

"Sorry," I whisper. "This doesn't normally happen."

It has over the last five years. But she doesn't need to know that.

She waves me off. "Don't worry, I've had people cry on me a whole lot more about a whole lot less. Just head on home and try to get some rest before we get to work tomorrow."

It feels like a walk of shame to get to my car. Even when no one's around, I feel like the eyes of the whole town are on me—judging just how far I've fallen.

Maybe just more guilt about abandoning my parent's legacy, I think as I drive home.

Fuck, what if I never get over this? What if I sell the restaurant and spend the rest of my life hating myself for it? How do I fix that? It's not like I can call them from beyond the grave and ask for a blessing to move on with my life...

But maybe someone else could.

I take a sharp left turn at the next light, turning around. I have to talk to Paige.

———

IT TAKES twenty minutes of driving and another thirty waiting in front of the back office, but I finally get Paige sitting with me, eating popsicles behind her bakery. Just like we used to as kids on my front porch.

"Alright we're dripping in popsicle juice and I'm beyond curious as to what the fuck is going on," Paige says. "So spill. You and lover boy finally running off into the sunset? Do I get to plan a shotgun wedding because you're both raging attention-phobes?"

"What? No." I say, blushing. "We're not even dating."

"Okay...then what is it?"

"I'm selling the restaurant," I say.

She blinks at me for a moment before continuing to suck on her popsicle.

"Well…"

"Well what?" she asks.

"Well what do you think?"

She sighs, closing her eyes. "If that's what you want...then I'm happy for you."

That...wasn't what I was expecting. I thought she'd be...I don't know. More enthusiastic? Prouder of me for doing something for myself for once. What the fuck?

Light rain droplets start to hit us from overhead.

"That's it?" I say

She rolls her eyes. "What do you want me to say? 'Oh, you're completely abandoning the only thing left of your family AND this entire town, Kaitlynn? That's so exciting!'"

"Fuck, I don't mean…" I sputter. "You don't have to be...excited about it. But I thought you wanted me to be happy."

"I do, Katy. Honest to God I do," Paige says. "But wanting what's best for you doesn't make this suck any less."

"Paige, c'mon...you know how miserable I've been here," I say.

She laughs. "This again."

"It's true!" I say. "Since they left, there's nothing left for me here—"

"Goddammit, Katy, they were my parents too!" She shouts.

I gape, looking her in the eyes. They're so red and watery, like they've been meaning to cry for years but haven't yet. Fuck.

Paige wipes tears away from her face, furiously. "You were grieving, and I thought...that's okay. They were your biological parents. Of course, it was going to be harder on you. I have Mom and Dad but...thought we could talk shit out once you got better..."

She starts to tremble. "...But then things didn't get better, and I kept offering to help. I kept telling you, you needed to get out there again, live your fucking life. Stop waiting for them to come back as if they just went out on a date. I—you just kept pushing me away...I convinced you to take the restaurant away from Kelsey. I shouldn't have. You were trying to make it in Atlanta. I shattered your dreams."

"Paige..." I say quietly, my lip trembling.

"I felt so guilty for so long," she said with a tired laugh. "Like 'fuck me for ruining Kaitlynn's big city dreams by dragging her back home. Fuck me for trapping her in this goddamn place when she can't wait to get away from me and everyone here.'"

I close the distance between us, hugging her tightly. My popsicle is forgotten as I let it fall to the concrete. The rain begins to pound on us harder, soaking us completely.

"I'm sorry, Paigy Cakes for making you feel like you trapped me. You advised me, but I'm the one who chose coming back. I made the choice," I whisper as she sobs into my chest. "I'm so, so sorry. I'm sorry for not being there for you."

We stay there for a while, tears spilling silently as we cling to each other. I don't remember the last time we talked about something that wasn't our jobs or guys or even Kelsey. When did I start to let my best friend down so hard?

"Fuck, you can leave if you want," she whispers at some point. "You don't have to hate your home to leave it...but yeah, if you spend too long forcing yourself to stay home of course you'd hate it...But I miss you, okay? I'll miss you, so much."

It hits me, suddenly, how much I've given up over the last few years. Not just physically but mentally and emotionally. I've slipped so far away from anything resembling happiness that I can barely recognize myself. I've sacrificed so much of myself and for what?

My sister is gone. One of my best friends almost died and never told me. My other best friend spent years quietly trying to fix the broken pieces of me that I refused to fix. I was so...obsessed with focusing on what was wrong with my life and what I couldn't control that I forgot there was still a lot about me that I can control.

I let despair take over my entire personality. I let myself take it out on everyone else without accepting any of the fault. I've been so stubborn in my self-wallowing that I hurt myself and her. One of the most important people in my life, in the process.

"I'll be better, okay," I whisper to Paige as I hold her closer. "You don't have to carry both of us anymore, okay? I got you too."

She nods through sniffles, her lips twitching slightly as she buries her head in my neck.

"We'll figure things out. Us, the restaurant...everything," I say.

"Okay," she says. "...I meant it though, Katy. Whatever you need, we'll do it. It's going to be okay. You can sell it; we can start from scratch. Paige and Katy cakes."

We laugh as the sun peeks out between two rain clouds, brightening the whole world. It feels like the weight of existing as a Blythe in Knox Ridge has been lifted off my shoulders.

"Yeah," I say. "It will be fine."

For the first time in years, I know it's true.

AFTER SITTING on the curb and talking to Paige for a while, I head home for the night. I'll reassess in the morning and see what our next move is going to be. Paige is right, the Blythe legacy is just as much hers as it is mine...and Ollie's for that matter. Selling the restaurant is a decision we should make together.

My parents would want that.

This day has been so long and not at all what I had imagined or I wanted—I miss Oliver already.

Is that crazy? We have to fix our shit. I need to make peace with what I feel and what he won't. Work with my emotions. It's going to be hard when I feel so empty without him. How can that be true?

It's only been a day.

How could I miss someone like a part of me?

I sigh as I lock my car. Maybe Ollie is like Knox Ridge...always a part of me whether I realize it or not. I just have to understand that he's a friend and nothing else.

Once I'm on my floor, I notice someone sitting in the hall, leaning against the door to my apartment. He's fidgeting with his phone. I step closer, realizing—

"Ollie?" I say out loud. "Is that you?"

Oliver looks up, standing almost immediately.

"Who else would it be?" he asks. "What's his face? Juan? Julio?"

"It's Javier, and no," I say, scowling.

"Where have you been?" he asks.

I cross my arms. "Not that it's any of your business but...talking to Paige. There were some things I needed to hear...but enough about me, why are you here, Ollie?"

"Because you decided to just drop everything and sell the restaurant without even talking to me," he says. "How could you?"

"You're right," I say. "I should have talked to you before the realtor. I'm sorry you had to find out the way you did."

He stares at me like I've grown a second head. "...Really?"

I smirk sadly. "Yes, really. You're a Blythe. You've always been a Blythe. You get a say too."

Ollie straightens up. "...Okay good. Because you can't do it alone, Kit Kat—"

"I know," I say.

"And you need to be able to accept help—"

"I know," I say again.

"Because there's only so much one person can do, and it's okay not to be a superhero.

You're still a hero to me...and everyone in this town."

"Yeah, okay, message received," I say with a smile. "How long were you rehearsing that?"

He blushes. "Just the last fifteen minutes. I'm not a touchy-feely kind of guy."

I shake my head, holding back another laugh. "It's okay. I'm bad with this stuff too."

"But I want us to talk," he says firmly. "I don't want to leave things the way they were."

I sigh, shrugging as I stare at our shoes. Part of me wants to crawl into a hole and never come out. But Oliver has been waiting for me to talk, so it's the least I can give him.

So, I open my door and let him inside before we get to the reality check part of this conversation. We don't need everyone to know our business.

"Okay. How did we leave things, Ollie?"

"Up in the air," he says. "I apologized for being an idiot. I thought we were going to work things out. That we were going to start something. That you were going to give the restaurant and me another chance. But I woke up, and you were gone."

I feel my breath catch in my throat. "Well, since it was a onetime thing between us," I admit. "Why stay for the awkward conversation? So, I get it you know. You said, it was casual."

Perking up, I continue waving my hand and staring at my shoes. "Obviously after reading the letters you know how I felt...feel. It'll be a process to move on—"

"A, I said casual by mistake. I meant simple. And, B, if someone tells you he loves you," he interrupts me. "I think that's more than a onetime thing; and I'm guessing you don't know it as you presumed."

When I look up at him, he's got a smile that says he thinks this is funny, but his eyes are timid. I take a step closer, shrugging.

"I thought I made that part up," I say. "I'm a little rusty at being around people who aren't my employees or Paige. Maybe I just...don't know what that word sounds like anymore?"

He closes the gap between us, brushing my hair away from my face.

"Okay," he says. "Why don't we try this again? Kaitlynn Blythe?"

"Yeah?" I say quietly.

He kisses my forehead, and then kisses my lips softly.

"I love you," he says. "I really fucking love you. I think I've been in love with you since the moment you taught me to chase fireflies and the magic within them."

I bite my lip hard enough to feel a bruise already forming. Yep, I'm definitely awake. This definitely isn't a dream.

"I guess I should tell you that, uh, I love you too," I murmur.

He laughs like he's trying to force it. Like he's trying to keep things casual and easy for me. No, I shake my head. He wants this. He's been waiting for me for God knows how long just to make sure I understand he loves me.

"I really fucking love you, Oliver Tanner," I say again, with more conviction.

This time, I kiss him. It's harsh and it's desperate laden with years' worth of pining, sorrow, and regret rolled into one. I want him to feel how much I've missed him; how much I've been dying to have this.

Eventually, we have to break apart to get some air. I hear someone laughing. It takes me a minute to realize it's me. I laugh harder.

He looks at me with a concerned smile. "What?"

"This is nice. Better than I imagined."

His smile broadens. "Well you deserve to have whatever you

want."

"You think so?" I say quietly. "Even after I fucked up the restaurant so badly?"

"It's not your fault that the restaurant is this way," he says. "I know you want to pursue your real dreams, and you want to keep Blythe's open. You shouldn't have to choose. You deserve both. Let me help you."

There he goes again, I think, *promising the world.*

"You make it sound so easy," I say. "Like the soul of that place wasn't crushed out of it five years ago."

He caresses my cheek. "We're not your parents. But we can make Blythe's work in a different way. You can do your own show from the restaurant without having to move out of here. The kitchen will be brand new by next week. We can really make this work."

"You think so?" I ask.

He nods. "I know so."

"What makes you think you're so smart, Ollie?"

He smiles sadly. "I was raised by some pretty smart people. And you know what one of the smartest women I've ever known once told me at my lowest point?"

I shake my head, a lump forming in the back of my throat.

"Maybe we're not what you wanted or had in mind when you imagined your life," he says softly. "But we're what you've got. And we love you, alright? Don't push away the people who love you. You're hurting? Let us help carry the load."

I bite my lip, eyes watering. "Who was that?"

"Your mom," he says.

"Figures," I say, sobbing. Missing her so much and wishing she was with me because..."She always knew what to say."

"She was smart...and right. Don't give up because you feel alone, Kit Kat. We've got you. Everyone in this town loves you."

I shudder as he kisses my forehead. How can he be like this? So optimistic and determined? Ollie believes in Blythe's as much as my parents used to—as I did when I took it over. My eyes flicker up to his. They're burning like embers left over from a fire, refusing to go out.

He kisses me again, and I realize something. Maybe all this time he wasn't fighting for me to believe in the restaurant. Maybe he was fighting for me to believe in...myself.

I feel something slip from the corner of my eye. Oliver brushes it away with his thumb. I start laughing again because this kind of stuff doesn't happen to me. People don't support me, or ask what they can do for me. He squeezes me into a hug, tethering me to the present.

He's been trying so hard since he arrived to get me with the program...to get me feeling alive again. The least I can do is trust him.

"Okay," I say quietly. "Let's do this."

"YOU ASSHOLES BETTER HAVE coffee and a good reason to be waking me up early," Paige says as she gets into my car the next morning.

It's five thirty am, later than I normally wake up but a bit earlier for Paige now that she has another baker working the morning shift.

Ollie's driving, because he insists its part of his master plan.

"Don't ask me, it's his plan,"

"Whatever," she says with a yawn and eyes our intertwined hands. "Nice of you to finally get your head out of your ass, Ollie-pop. Let's hope your friend does the same soon."

He chuckles. "Not my business but I'm sure he will, Paigy Cakes."

"God, I hate you both," she says with a smile. "So where are we going? Your elopement?"

"You're such a voyeur—" I say at the same time as Ollie says "—Not just yet."

Paige cackles. "I miss this. You're just too fucking easy to mess with."

I blush. "Takes one to know one."

I know this town like the back of my hand so I realize quickly that we're headed towards Blythe's. I'm surprised, however, about the dozens of people I see walking in the direction we're driving. People from all over town, some in their work clothes and some in their pajamas, are walking toward our restaurant.

"What the fuck," Paige says, voicing my thoughts.

When we pull up to the restaurant, there are even more people out front. Some of the carpenters and foremen are shouting directions. People are moving in and out of the building. I can see people going upstairs to the second-floor storage. A bunch of teenagers are arranging paint cans with the art teachers and a few interior designers. Some people are bustling out of the restaurant with rolls of carpet.

I look at Ollie as he parks the car. "What is this?"

Ollie looks out at the yard. "I realized you couldn't save the restaurant...and Paige was smart enough to know it wasn't going to work if anyone tried alone."

"To be fair, the same goes for if I did it alone," Paige says.

"So..." Ollie says as he opens his car door. "I made a few calls to a few friends, asked if they could help us get Blythe's through some hard times. You know, return the kindness and investments that your family put into the city for decades."

We get out of the car. I'm dumbfounded by the crowds here...that are still growing.

"Who'd you call?" I ask as Ollie ushers Paige and me around the car.

"Everyone," Ollie says. "And they all invited people."

People smile and wave as Ollie corals us through their work.

"We got construction crews here. Carl's working as we agreed on the quote he gave you."

"Holy fuck, you got Carl?" I say.

Ollie shrugs. "The guy owes me too. Oh, and Frimston and the security guys came here to help too. Apparently, they all love your shepherd's pie."

I laugh as the sky starts to turn from black to dawn blue.

"It pays to know your customers," Paige says.

"Yes," Ollie says as he gets us up the stairs of the restaurant.

Someone hands Ollie a megaphone.

"But when you're the kind of people that give the shirt off your back, people remember that," Ollie says into the megaphone. "It took me five hours yesterday to get through...even fifty phone calls. Because every person in Knox Ridge has a story about Kaitlynn, Paige, Josey, Richard, Cynthia, or Patrice Blythe—and how they never gave up giving back to Knox Ridge, a home they love so much that they adopted everyone in it."

The crowd laughs. I feel Ollie's hand squeeze mine tight as Paige laughs into my shoulder.

"Cynthia used to tell me, 'it isn't easy being a Blythe,'" Ollie says. "She was right. It's hard work to give the kind of love that doesn't die and the kind of community pride that lets you reach out to your neighbor like family."

I feel tears go down my cheeks. Love was in everything my parents did. Ollie's right, Knox Ridge isn't just the place where my parents died. It's the people we loved and cared for along the way.

"But it's work worth doing for people who would and have done the same for us, sevenfold," he says. "So, let's get to work. We can make this place better for the future generations of Knox Ridge."

The sun comes up for the first time in years.

TWENTY-SIX

Oliver

WITH THE CREW, the volunteers and the security guys who came to help, it takes us another week to bring Blythe's into the next century. HIB not only helped with the renovations but also with the security. Bradley was right, I didn't just accept a job, I joined a family.

This family comes with connections. By the end of the week, he flies in his brother in-law who is a movie and television producer to chat with Kaitlynn.

"If I wasn't a married man, I'd marry your cobbler," he says as he tries Nana's famous peach cobbler.

Then, he turns to look at Mason and says, "tell my family I won't come back home."

"If the restaurant was open, I'd throw together some homemade vanilla ice cream," Kaitlynn half jokes.

"I watched some of your old tapes," Matthew says, wiping his mouth and washing the cobbler down with sweet iced tea. "You're good. I like that sweet southern drawl and the sassiness you bring to the screen."

"You did?"

Matthew nods.

"We can set up your own channel. You and I can partner. You can stream from your social media, but every week, you have a show with me where you cook something that's exclusive to my streaming channel."

"What's the catch?"

"As I said, I'm offering this because I like what I saw, and this town is quaint. I don't want anything in return." He shakes his head. "We pay you for that one-hour episode a week. I help you get some big names to sponsor your 'kitchen' but I can't guarantee what you'll get. And … you send me cobbler every week."

"That's all?"

He nods.

"You're sure?"

"Yes," he assures her. "I'll get paid enough for the one-hour show. We can sit down with our lawyers and tune the details. I'm not paying much. Just enough, but you might be able to get a lot from those sponsorships. Becoming an Instagram and social media celebrity has its advantages. If you need help balancing that with your private life, I have people to help you."

"Ollie," she says, dumbfounded. "Did you hear that?"

"I heard, baby," I answer, pulling her tight and kissing the top of her head.

It warms my soul to see that smile again. The same that received me twenty-five years ago when dad had died, and we had to move to a new place where I didn't know anyone. My only comfort was Nana and Katy's smile. Now that she's coming back to life, it hits me how lost she had been.

The only comfort I have, is knowing that everything we're doing is bringing back my Katy.

"I WAS THINKING," I say, as we drive toward my house.

"It's scary to hear you say that, Oliver Tanner," she sighs.

"Well, now that we're done with Blythe's, I *think* we have to do the same with the house."

She puts her phone down and stares at me as I park the car in the garage.

"What do you mean?"

"Well, the place needs some TLC. It needs a new roof," I say.

She smiles. "A newer and bigger kitchen too."

I grin because she can see it. The possibilities that we can bring into the house. Making it our home.

"When do you want to start that?" she asks excitedly.

"We'll need to pack everything. Maybe Mom can come over to take what she wants. We can donate the furniture that still works and store the rest."

"Where would you stay?" she twists her lips, trying to hide the smile.

"I was hoping you have room in your bed for me," I say, winking at her.

"We might need a bigger bed, but I can invite you for an extended sleepover," she says with a sultry voice then her lips press close together to mine. "But first, are you working with those security guys?"

I nod. "It's something I can start once the restaurant is working the way we want. There's going to be an office in the house where I can work remote."

"Would you have to travel?" She says, and I can hear that uncertainty I heard the day I announced I'd enlist.

From everyone, she was the one who got it, even when she didn't like it.

"If it's required, it'll be short trips. They want me to lead from home. The only trips I want to take are with you. Remember that summer in Tybee island where you wanted to cruise along the ocean?"

"I was a kid."

"You were a dreamer. And you know what, we're going to make that happen. We will cruise around the world and we will come back home after discovering a new country or a new state. We always come home."

"Home," she repeats before I take her lips and kiss her deeply.

TWENTY-SEVEN

Kaitlynn

_____

I SHOULD'VE NEVER VOLUNTEERED to do this. Now that the reno is over, I'm in the middle of moving into Ollie's house. Almost a year after he came back home, the place is ready for us. While he's tampering with the internet connection and unpacking the equipment for his new office, I stupidly volunteered to help organize the shit he never got around to.

So of course, instead of unpacking, I'm rifling through his old letters again. I would feel bad about doing this if it weren't for the fact that we wrote these letters to each other.

So, there's nothing I haven't seen before.

And then I found this:

Kit Kat,

If you're reading this, I'm already gone. When they asked us to write these letters, the one person I wanted to make sure I said goodbye to was you. I don't know if you'll miss me, but I know I've been missing you every second of every day since I left. That was too many years ago.

Remember when we used to chase fireflies in my backyard? We trapped them in jars. You used to call them floating night lights, keeping the monsters away as they roamed the darkness. I would keep them on my nightstand, thinking about you. Because you were my own personal light, keeping everything else at bay. No matter what trouble I was in or what challenges we faced, you were always there next to me with a defiant smile.

During my deployments, our memories are my fireflies. They keep me going, reminding me just what I'm fighting for. For our safety, for our happiness, for you.

Every time you see a firefly, I want you to remember that you're a firefly in everyone's life. You love so much and bring warmth to every person you meet. I don't think you realize how much you help the people around you. You're a brilliance in the darkest nights, Kaitlynn Blythe.

Since I can't be the one to remind you, I hope you find someone who sees that in you. Someone who treasures you for the wonderful, beautiful woman that you are.

I will always love you. I wish I had said it before.

Forever yours,

Ollie

"WHAT ARE YOU READING NOW?" He pulls me into his embrace.

"You wrote me a letter in case you died," I sniff, crumbling, yet thankful that he's here, with me.

"Nothing happened. I'm here, Kit Kat. With you, and I plan to stay by your side forever."

"You think I'm a firefly." And to think I compare myself to a cicada. "Only you, Ollie."

"Baby, you're the best thing that's ever happened to me. You are my light, my lifeline, my everything."

"We're the best thing that happened to each other," I correct him.

"It's getting late," he says. "Come with me."

He grabs my hand and we walk toward the back of the house. There are two jars on top of the new patio table.

"What are we doing?" I ask when he hands me the jar.

"Chasing fireflies," he explains annoyed because what else do you do during summer with a mason jar?

"You never change, Ollie-pollie."

As I catch the fireflies, I remember Nana and my parents. I imagine them sitting by the porch on the new furniture we bought yesterday drinking iced tea while they watched us.

I still miss them, but now that Oliver is by my side, I've been able to grieve and move on from the pain. I remember them with love and miss them, yet, I'm happy they're now with Nana and Papa, and that they left together.

"You only got two," I tell Oliver when he's putting on the lid with holes.

"Well, they want to be alone," he says.

"Is that right?" I laugh, wondering why he'd do that. "They told you so?"

"As a matter of fact, yes. You see, this little guy just proposed to his beautiful lady. Now, what kind of man would I be if I add more fireflies when all he wants is to..." he smirks and wiggles his eyebrows. "Celebrate."

"You're so thoughtful, Tanner."

He hands over the jar, takes out a box from his pocket and bends on one knee.

I gasp in surprise, my heart beating fast and my body quivering with excitement. This can't be real.

He opens the box where a beautiful emerald surrounded by little diamonds peeks. Like perfect small kisses, guarding the green stone.

"Katy, you inspire me to complete myself. You don't judge me for my flaws. You see my jagged edges and still love me that way. You challenge me to be better, to see myself in ways that I never thought were possible. It's because of you that I believe in me. I love you for being imperfect in your own perfect way. I love you because you held my hand when I was lost and you shared your world with me without asking questions, accepting me as I am. I love you because you're the best person in the world.

"Kaitlynn Hope Blythe," he says, clearing his throat. "Would you do me the honor to become my wife, the mother of our children and my eternal companion?"

"Ollie," I say, sobbing while the fireflies flutter around us. I can feel my parents and Nana around too. "Of course, I want to be your wife."

Epilogue

Oliver

THE SUN SETS LAZILY over Knox Ridge. Spring is rolling over into summer. The days are getting longer as they melt one into one other. As I lie in my hammock, I take in the clouds flying overhead, tinted in reds and purples.

Two years ago, I returned to Knox Ridge without a plan or a goal. I knew something was calling me. It wasn't something, but someone. Kaitlynn. My wife.

We worked hard to transform Blythe's into a restaurant we could be proud of and that the customers would enjoy. Once the kitchen was ready, Kaitlynn began to record her cooking shows from our restaurant. As her viewership grew, so did our crowd. Daily we receive local patrons and tourists that come from all over the world to enjoy her delicious food.

Blythe's has become exactly what I imagine Richard and Cynthia would've wanted it to be. I know in my heart that they are proud of the woman Kaitlynn has become. I'm proud of her, of *us*.

My job at the restaurant is to make sure that everything outside the kitchen works properly. After hours, I work with Striker and the team of HIB doing private security. Our lives and our business run like a well-oiled machine, and for the past couple of months we've been able to take every other night and every Saturday off too.

It's been a process for both of us, but we've learned that life is more than the job. It's also about enjoying yourself and taking a few moments to be with those you love. I roll over sluggishly, watching Kaitlynn from across the backyard. She's been fretting over a fucking Instagram photo for ten minutes already. Being a social media icon never ends. There's always something new and amazing that she wants to share with her fans.

It's driving me nuts, but what can I do? Kaitlynn always gets what she wants. Not that I could deny her anything after she asks.

The farther the sun gets from us, the more fireflies start to peek out of their hiding spots. My lips twitch into a smile. Kaitlynn's always beautiful, but these are her kind. She glows more when she's around fireflies.

"Can you please put that phone away?" I say finally. "We have the night off."

"Can you be a little more patient?" she calls out mockingly. "I'm trying to get the perfect shot."

I sit up, curious. She starts walking toward me. Her footsteps are deliberate, determined. Her wedding ring glinting against our porch lights.

"Of what?" I ask, humoring her.

She stops about a foot in front of the hammock. At this point, it looks like that camera's aimed right at me.

She smiles shyly. "I'm pregnant."

My heart stops. I hear the camera shutter go off on her phone. She giggles. The sound of it brings blood rushing back to my head.

"#Hesgoingtobeadad #BabyTanner #KnoxRidgelife #Blythes #foodforthesoul #babyfirefly," she recites the hashtags.

"You're serious?" I ask quietly.

She nods as she closes the gap between us, wrapping her arms around my neck.

"What do you think of that, Daddy?" she says playfully.

I know she's trying to tease me. It only makes me smile broader. I kiss the air out of her lungs, saying everything I wish I had the words for.

For how much I love and worship her, how thankful I am every morning to wake up next to her, how she fills every corner of my life with light and joy. She's all I've ever wanted, and some days I can't believe it. She's too good to be true.

"I think it's perfect," I murmur before kissing her again.

There's nowhere I'd rather be but right here at home, by her side.

Kaitlynn

I ARRIVE HOME AROUND NINE. The show went a little longer than I expected. When I agreed to this *sixth-year anniversary live*, I didn't think about the Q&A. Even when we limited it, we had a long line of questions and as usual, I took my time to answer them. Some of them were about cooking a specific dish. Others about my family.

Every time I'm on the show, I bring up Mom or Nana. Other's it's Dad. I like to share the town history or my own family history while I'm cooking. Other times, I talk about Cindy, our little firefly.

Mostly, when I'm doing a segment for children. I explain how Nana used to teach me how to do simple things, just the way I do with Cindy, my baby girl. I chuckle. She's not a baby anymore. She's four and sometimes she scares me because she sounds like a grown up already.

It's still a tricky balance to keep my private life away from the public but we manage. I slip off my shoes and place them right next to Ollie's. The house is dark, but I can hear the giggles coming all the way down from upstairs. The little firefly is still awake. Let's hope Damon is in bed. He's an unhappy toddler when he stays awake past his bedtime.

Carefully, trying not to make much noise I climb the stairs. When I reach Cindy's room, I smile. She's holding the old picture book. Next to her is Ollie and he's holding Damon's sleepy body.

"It's past your bedtime, young lady," I whisper.

"Daddy is telling me the story," she says, brushing me away because she knows she can do whatever she wants with her dad.

Oliver is as good of a father as Dad was with us. He adores our kids and they adore him back.

"Again?" I look at her nightstand where the mason jar lies. It's empty. "You didn't go out to the yard tonight?"

"It was raining," Oliver tells me, kissing Cindy's forehead. "We can try again tomorrow, okay?"

"Okay, Daddy," she nods and yawns. "I love you forever."

"I love you too, baby firefly," he says giving her a hug and rising from the bed.

"Welcome home, baby." He brushes my lips with his. "I'm going to put this little guy in his crib. Mind if you pray with her."

"Hey," I greet him and kiss Damon's little head.

"Can I see your show tomorrow, Mommy?"

"Of course, baby. Why don't we say our prayers and then go to sleep?"

We kneel in front of the bed and she leads like every night. "Thank you for granting us another day. Please bless everyone in this house. Keep Daddy safe when he goes in his missions—and all his team. Keep Mommy safe. Bless Damon, Nana Josey, Papa Toby, auntie Paige, Uncle Striker, my cousin Patrice. Make sure Little Johnny arrives soon so Damon has a friend to play with. Bless our family who are in heaven and the town of Knox Ridge. Amen."

"And take care of Cindy Lou, may her heart keep being sweet, and dreams always come true. Amen," I say.

"Should we pray for aunt Kelsey?"

"Kelsey?" I ask curiously. We don't speak of her in the house. "Yes, I found a picture of her and Dad told me she's my aunt too, but she lives far away."

"Yes, let's pray for her too, sweetie. Let's pray that God keeps her safe and her family too."

After I finish tucking her in, I go pass the nursery and make sure my sweet boy is asleep and say a little prayer to keep him safe. Every night, I ask my parents and grandparents to look after my babies and my husband.

"You talked about Kelsey?" I ask Ollie.

"She found an old picture that you had in the closet." He shrugs.

It's sad that the only memory I have of my sister is an old photograph. That I have no idea where or how she is doing, because she decided not to talk to me again. Not if I wasn't going to give her what she deserves. The last time we spoke she insisted Blythe's was hers too.

"I thought she was going to change, you know."

"Baby, you have to let it go. Family stays together, those who look for you when they know you can give them something aren't family," he reminds me, giving me a hug. "How was the show?"

We talk about the show, while I get ready for bed. He tells me that he spent almost all evening telling our daughter the story of how Olli-pop the firefly came to Knox Ridge, then he left but came back when his firefly wanted him back.

"That's your story?" I laugh.

"It's just part of our story. A tale we'll continue building every day," he says, and he kisses me hard.

After all these years, his kisses feel just like the first one. Hungry, passionate, sweet, loving. Very slowly, with hands and mouths we unwrapped each other. He lifts me high as he thrusts himself inside me. Our mouths fuse, our hearts melt. We become one, like we do every night. Our souls play, just as our tongues and bodies.

Before I fall asleep, like I do every night, I say a thank you for sending him back home, safe, to me.

Dear Reader,

Thank you so much for spending some time with Kaitlynn and Oliver in Knox Ridge. Last year, I released this book through the collection Cards of Love. When I decided to rebrand it, I wanted to give you a little more of their world and their lives.

As always, I want to thank you for accepting a little piece of me through my stories and characters.

Please, after finishing the book and if you enjoyed it, do me a big favor and leave a review. Let other readers know about it and spread the word. I love to hear from readers, so don't hesitate to message me.

Love,

Claudia xo

Acknowledgments

Pardon my memory. It's pretty shifty. If I forget to mention some-one, please know it's not intentional. My brain has low retention.

First and foremost, I'd like to thank God for all the blessings in my life. For my family, my friends, my readers, and my health. Also, for letting me do what I love the most writing stories.

To my family, thank you for all your support, even when most of you are thousands of miles away from me. My wonderful and loving husband. The best real-life boyfriend and love I could've been given. He's not only my partner but my everything.

We always keep going, no matter what kind of obstacles we find along the way, we fight them together and continue our journey.

To our beautiful children. The light of my life.

To my alpha readers: Yolanda, Patricia, and Michelle, who helped me with the original novella. I hope you like what I did with this story.

Thank you to Karen, for giving me a hand for the past month. Hopefully, you'll want to stick around forever, or something like that.

Thank you to Danielle, Mara, Paulina, and Dana for helping me shape this book.

Thank you, Hang Le, for this gorgeous cover. For all your patience and your friendship.

Thank you so much to Natasha Tomic for letting me do the cover reveal of Chasing Fireflies on her blog, and for always being there when I need her.

Kristi, my BFL and cheerleader. Thank you for always being there for me.

My amazing ARC team, girls you are an essential part of my team. Thank you for always being there for me.

To my Chicas! Thank you so much for your continuous support and for being there for me every day!

Thank you to all the bloggers who help me spread the word about my books. Thank you never cuts it just right, but I hope it's enough.

To the readers, you guys are everything. Thank you so much for taking the time to read my words, spreading the word, and sending me messages about how much you love my characters or how the stories have touched your lives. It's because of you that I can continue doing what I love.

Thank you for everything.

All my love,

Claudia xoxo

About the Author

Claudia is an award-winning, *USA Today* bestselling author. She lives in Colorado, working for a small IT. She has three children and manages a chaotic household of two confused dogs, and a wonderful husband who shares her love of all things geek. To survive she works continually to find purpose for the voices flitting through her head, plus she consumes high quantities of chocolate to keep the last threads of sanity intact.

To find more about Claudia:
   www.claudiaburgoa.com

Also by Claudia Burgoa

Uncut

Undefeated

Decker the Halls

Made in the USA
Las Vegas, NV
19 November 2022

59814483R10132